SUNDAY

E. L. TODD

Fallen Publishing

Sunday

CHAPTER ONE

Buried Six Feet Under

Kyle

I stopped in mid-sentence as I addressed the jury, driving my point home. My confident and calm exterior disappeared the moment I saw her standing there, a look of horror on her face. Her eyes were coated with tears, and beneath that moisture was the heaviest look of betrayal I'd ever seen. There would be no forgiveness—and there would be no forgetting.

She marched out of the courtroom, moving as fast as she could without running. Her heels echoed on the hardwood floor because the room was so silent. Her departure took up everyone's focus. And everyone stared at me, trying to make sense of what just happened.

My first impulse was to chase after her and explain the situation. Walking into the courtroom and seeing me as the prosecutor must have been jarring—and nauseating.

But I couldn't do anything about it.

I was in the middle of a trial, and there was no excuse grand enough I could make to storm out. And if I did, it would make me look bad. I couldn't afford to ruin my image to the jury, not when Audrey and Rose had so much on the line.

I did my best to cover it up. "I'm sorry, everyone. That was Rose...Peter's previous victim. She came her to see justice, but looking at him was too much. She had to go."

Every member of the jury looked at the door like they suspected she might return.

I adjusted my tie and took a second to remember my train of thought. A witness was still on the stand, the waitress who waited on Audrey and Peter that terrible night. I wasn't done with my point, and I had to keep going.

So I did.

***

Keeping up the same demeanor, I slowly walked out of the courtroom like I had nowhere else to be. Everyone else filed out, returning to their lives outside the courtroom.

Even though I seemed calm to everyone else, I was dying inside. My heart was pounding so hard I thought it might explode like a land mine. I hated myself for hurting Rose, for allowing her to find out this way. I needed to set the record straight, to explain my actions—and lack of actions.

When I was finally on the sidewalk and away from witnesses, I kicked my ass into gear and picked up the speed. I practically ran all the way to her apartment, migrating through the sea of foot traffic. If she wasn't at her apartment, I didn't know where else to go. I would call her but I suspected that would be pointless.

I took the stairs two at a time until I reached her floor. I didn't bother with the elevator because I could run faster than that ancient piece of machinery. When I arrived at her door I was out of breath and covered in sweat. "Rose?" I knocked on the door harder than I meant to, shaking the wood because I was so anxious.

There wasn't a sound inside.

She had to be there. Where else would she go? If she planned on going somewhere she would have come by the apartment to grab her things. I was only an hour behind her. "Please open the door, Rose."

Still nothing.

What I was about to do was immoral on so many levels but I was desperate. I grabbed a paperclip from my satchel and picked the lock until it came clean. The door drifted open, revealing a quiet apartment with no one inside.

I walked in and shut the door behind me, locking it just the way it was before I picked it. She wasn't anywhere in sight. It didn't seem like she came here in a rush either. When I inspected her bedroom it didn't seem like anything had been taken. She must have gone somewhere else because she knew I would come here.

Maybe she was at her office.

I sat on the couch and set my satchel down. If I chased her all over the city she would just run. If I stayed in one spot and waited for her to come to me, I would have the chance to talk to her.

It was wrong to wait it out inside her apartment, somewhere she felt safe, but I was desperate. And you know the saying, desperate times call for desperate measures.

I leaned my back on the couch and tried to steady my racing heart. The anxiety was getting to me, swallowing me up. Rose meant the world to me. She'd become an integral part of my soul. When she told me she loved me, I felt complete. The search for my future wife had officially ended.

I couldn't lose her.

***

Late that night, she came home.

The apartment was dark because I didn't turn on any lights. If I weren't so upset, I probably would have fallen asleep since I sat there for so many hours. The key jiggled in the door then she stepped inside.

She assumed she was alone because she shut the door and tossed her purse on the table. Then she ran her fingers through her hair, releasing a painful sigh that went all the way into my chest. She stared at the table before she closed her eyes.

I didn't need to hear her tell me how much I hurt her. I could see it that very moment.

She released her hair then grabbed a bottle of water from the fridge, moving unnaturally slow. The life seemed to have left her body, like she had no will to do anything.

Now I didn't know what to do. I didn't want to startle her, but not making my presence known might scare her even more. I rose from the couch and turned to her, deciding to clear my throat.

She turned around and spotted me in the darkness. "Agh!" Her water left her hands and fell to the ground, pouring out everywhere. She immediately backed up and reached for a knife in a drawer, terrified for her life.

"Rose, it's me." I flipped the switch on the wall so the lights would come on. "It's just me." I raised my hands in the air, giving her a gesture of surrender. "I'm sorry I scared you, sweetheart."

She gripped the knife tightly in her hand before she dropped it on the counter.

I lowered my hands, still terrified of what was going to happen next.

"Get. Out." Her body shook as she stared me down, the unbridled rage escaping from the back of her throat. "Get out or I'll call the police. I doubt it'll look good for your record if you're caught harassing a former client."

I didn't expect her to take this well, but I hadn't anticipated it being this bad either. "Rose, let me explain—"

"Explain what? That you're a liar? A predator?"

"Whoa...what?" My voice could no longer stay calm, not when I got that kind of accusation. "A predator? What the hell is that supposed to mean?"

"You know what happened to me and you manipulated me into getting what you wanted."

"That's the stupidest thing I've ever heard."

"Is not," she snapped. "You knew I'd been raped so you did everything necessary to get my walls to come down. And then you took advantage of me once you got me to trust you. Maybe it's not rape, but you certainly tricked me into doing something I wouldn't have done if I'd known otherwise."

I'd never been so hurt by words in my life. "That's not how it was, Rose. You know that."

"Get out of my apartment." She pointed to the door. "I mean it, Kyle."

"I just want to talk about this. I didn't manipulate you into doing anything. For the first two months of this relationship, I didn't even know what happened. When I found out, everything made sense. I did what I could to get you to confide in me but nothing worked. I wanted

8

you to come to me on your own terms. I waited and waited but you were never ready. And the only reason why I wanted you to tell me was so I could show you it doesn't change anything."

She crossed her arms over her chest and refused to look at me. "I don't understand how you could go on for so long without telling me you knew...I'm so embarrassed."

"There's no reason to be embarrassed." How could she possibly think it would change her image?

"That whole time we were together you knew what happened to me. I thought I could have a fresh start, be with a man who saw me as beautiful—"

"I've always thought that—before and after."

She shook her head, the tears starting to bubble up. "And then you slept with me without telling me..."

"You didn't tell me either." This was a two-way street. "I was going to say something before we...were together...but then you told me you loved me. When I heard those words, nothing else mattered. What does it matter where we've both been if we love each other? The past is irrelevant."

"I was going to tell you that night but then you said you loved me back...and I just forgot about it."

"Then we're both guilty of the same thing." And there was no reason to have this fight at all.

"I would have told you sooner but I was afraid of losing you..." She sniffed quietly then wiped her eyes with the back of her forearm.

"Like you could ever lose me." The distant pain in my chest started to rumble. I could feel it spread everywhere in my body—including my heart.

"I was afraid you would look at me differently."

"Never."

She took a deep breath, the kind that was painful, and then she looked at me again. "But you have no valid excuse. You purposely misled me so you could get what you wanted."

"No. I didn't tell you because I was afraid it would push you away."

"The fact you lied about it for so long is what has pushed me away."

Just when I thought we might reconcile, the conversation took a dangerous turn. "Rose, I understand why you're upset. It's shocking, to say the least. But I promise you, I've never had any sinister intent toward you. I wanted you to come to me on your own terms."

She turned her gaze to the floor, shutting me out.

"Sweetheart."

She leaned against the counter, keeping the table between us.

"I knew there was something between us the moment we met. When you walked into that restaurant, I was yours. After that moment, I couldn't stop thinking about you. As time went on, I became more obsessed. I could never figure out why—until I found out what happened. Don't you think it's a strange coincidence that my sister went through the exact same thing? What are the odds of that?"

She slowly turned her head my way, but her eyes were still impenetrable.

"I don't think that's a coincidence," I continued. "And that's when I fell even harder for you. I understand what you went through. I understand the burden you carry. What better man could you possibly be with than me?" That was a solid argument, one she couldn't possibly deny.

"Or maybe you just like weak women."

Now that pissed me off. "Weak? Who said anything about being weak? My sister wasn't weak. What happened to her was a crime of violence. And you aren't weak either. That's not how I see you."

She kept the space between us, still in the opposite corner of the apartment. She stood next to the knife on the counter like it comforted her, giving her some strength against me if she needed it.

The sight broke my heart.

"I can't get past this, Kyle..."

"There's nothing to get past. What happened to you occurred long before we met. Our relationship is based on so much more."

"It was based on trust—which no longer exists."

12

I wasn't losing her. I refused to let that happen. "And what should I have done? Confronted you the moment I found out? Brought up a subject you weren't ready to discuss? What would that have accomplished?"

She was silent like she didn't have an answer. "I would have known what I was dealing with. Now I know I kissed you and did stuff with you while you were thinking of that the entire time."

"Thinking of that?" I asked quietly. "Rose, I never think about it. I can't think about it because it kills me inside. Do you have any understanding of how much it hurts me?" Every time I considered what happened to her I was no longer a man. I fell into broken pieces. "I lock it up deep in the back of my mind, trying to forget about it. But when I'm with you, it doesn't cross my mind. I see the woman I love—and nothing else." I stepped around the couch, needing to decrease the distance between us.

She stiffened against the counter. "Don't come any closer to me."

I immediately stopped.

"You still should have told me."

"And it would have chased you off."

"Yes...it probably would." She tightened her arms around her chest, cutting me off even more.

"Then you understand why I didn't take that route."

"We were doomed either way, Kyle. At least if you took that route I would have gotten out of this relationship sooner."

It was like she was trying to hurt me. "What would that solve? We would be miserable without each other."

"And now I'm miserable anyway," she whispered.

Now I was scared this wasn't just a fight. "Rose, I'm sorry I didn't tell you. But you must realize I'm in a terrible position. No matter what I do, I lose."

She stared at the ground.

"All that matters is, I love you. You love me. That's the end of the story."

"But it's not the end of the story. You're the attorney on Peter's trial. You were just never going to tell me?"

"I didn't want to say anything because I thought it might upset you."

She started to pace in the kitchen, growing flustered. "Of course it would upset me. But to keep it from me is unacceptable. Mark is the one who called me."

Goddammit, Mark. "I didn't want to drag you into this—until the case was over."

She gripped her skull. "Do you realize how insane this is? You're living a double life, one that I didn't even know about."

"No, I'm not. I was going to tell you everything—I just didn't know when."

"I just can't wrap my mind around this…"

"Look, this is what happened." I tried to keep my voice calm even though I was shaking. "Mark asked for my advice about the trial. When I looked through the file I saw your picture. That's when I figured everything out. Since he lost your case I took it on because I couldn't afford to lose this one. I have to make sure Peter goes to jail for the rest of his life. I took this case for you. I want to do the right thing—*for you.*"

She stopped walking, her hand covering her mouth.

"Rose, I'm—"

"That means you saw everything. Every picture and every description I made..."

Unfortunately. I read her account of that evening, of all the terrible things the men did to her. It was so disturbing it made me cry—in my own office. It was painful to read about it, so I could only imagine how painful it was to experience it. The fact Rose still continued on with her life, still smiled and laughed, was beyond me. "Yes."

She closed her eyes like she'd been stabbed.

"It was hard to read it. It was hard to know the truth. But you know what? It makes me realize how strong you are. Only a strong woman could come back from that and hold her head high. You should be proud of yourself."

"That I was raped by five guys?" she asked coldly.

"Don't twist my words around." There was nothing I hated more, as a man and a lawyer. "Most women don't recover from these sorts of things, but you have."

"Who said I recovered?"

"I did." She was a beautiful person when she was with me, happy and carefree. "Rose, you're unbroken when you're with me. You're happy. To me, that means you're healed."

"It's far more complicated than that..." She was drifting further away, escaping to a place where I couldn't follow.

I came closer to her, needing to hold her.

"I told you not to come near me." She took another step back, her hand held out.

I stopped, hating this situation even more. "Rose, I'm sorry. I'm sorry for all of this."

She turned her gaze out the window, her eyes still wet.

"Please forgive me. I love you, and I don't want to live without you." She was vital to my existence. I'd spent twelve years of my adult life going through women like toilet paper. I only used them for a moment before I threw them away. Francesca was the first person who meant something to me. But when I met Rose, it was different. She shined brighter than the sun, making every other woman become blurred in the shadows. She wasn't just the next one.

She was the one.

"I just...so many lies."

"None of them were malicious."

"I just can't believe that entire time you knew. Now I understand why you were so gentle with me, why you didn't think my behavior was odd. I feel stupid for not figuring it out sooner."

My hands were still shaking by my sides.

"Now everything was a lie. Everything was nothing like it seemed."

"That's not true," I whispered. "Everything was real—whether I knew or not."

"I can't trust you."

That hurt more than anything else. "Yes, you can. You can trust me more than anyone."

She pulled out the kitchen chair and sat down, unable to stand on her own two feet anymore. "I want you to leave."

"I'm not going anywhere." I wasn't leaving this apartment until we settled our differences.

She rested her elbows on the table with her face pressed into her hands. "I can't do this…"

"Yes, you can." I pulled out the chair and sat beside her but restrained myself from touching her.

"I just don't feel the same way anymore." She didn't pull her hands away. "Nothing is what I thought it was. And then you slept with me without telling me you know…and then you're the attorney on the case. I feel like I was in a dream and now I've finally woken up."

I felt sick. "Rose, no."

She finally pulled her hands down, revealing her wet tears. "It's just not the same anymore. I don't trust you. I feel like I've been played—played hard."

"That's not how it was—"

"But that's how I feel."

"Rose—"

"Just go…" When she blinked more tears emerged. "If I'd known you'd known I wouldn't have slept with you. So I feel like I was tricked into doing something I wouldn't have done otherwise. And that's something you can never take back."

I couldn't believe this was happening. I wanted to argue she did the same thing to me when she didn't tell me the truth. But in my heart, I knew she was right. "I love you. That's something that's never changed. That's real and true—always."

"I believe you…"

Finally, some hope. "Then give me another chance."

"That's not possible. You can't have a redo in a situation like this. It just can't be done."

"That's not fair…"

"I know it's not." She sniffed and wiped her eyes with a napkin. "But that's how it has to be."

I felt my hands shake on the table, feeling the pain shoot all the way down to my stomach. Everything hurt. It was a new realm of pain.

"I really did love you, Kyle. But this isn't something I can get over. This isn't something I can move past. It changes everything—changes us." She clutched the tissue against her lips, the tears sliding down her cheeks. The apartment suddenly felt cold, like all the joy, hope, and love had been sucked out of it.

Or maybe it was just sucked out of me.

Sunday

CHAPTER TWO

On My Own

Kyle

I'd been depressed a lot in my life, but this had to be the worst. I lost Rose over something I couldn't control. No matter what action I took, it was the wrong one.

And that was unfair.

I hoped taking a step back would give her time to calm down and see reason. Or maybe it would give her enough time to realize that she loved me and couldn't live without me—the same way I felt about her.

When I pursued her, the wound was still fresh. She was bleeding all over the place, trailing it everywhere she

23

went. Giving her time to heal was the smartest move right now.

I had to keep my distance.

In my heart, I knew she would come back to me.

The case was my priority at the moment, and I couldn't lose my focus. Not only did Rose's justice sit on the line—but so did Audrey's. There were other victims of Peter's, ones that hadn't come forward—I was sure of it. There was a lot at stake. And I couldn't afford to lose the game.

Sitting in court was a great distraction from my break up with Rose. When I was this focused on another matter I was able to breathe. For that time period, it didn't seem like we were apart at all. My energy was entirely focused on the man sitting across the room.

Audrey was quiet the entire time, and she refused to take the stand and give her testimony. That was her right, but it did hurt us. If the jury could hear about the events directly from her mouth, there was no way they could doubt her story. Despite that evidence, Audrey refused to budge.

But I would still win this case.

***

I sat at my kitchen table for nearly three hours, the beer beside me untouched. I rested my face against my outstretched arm, leaning over the table like I was falling asleep in class.

I stared into my living room, noting the dark furniture and the black TV. Rose used to come over and watch basketball with me. We'd share a pizza and make fun of the opposing team playing against The Warriors. It was times like that when she was truly happy.

And I lost it.

Now I was alone, sitting in my apartment without anything to do. I wondered what she was doing, if she were thinking about me just the way I was thinking about her.

Did she miss me?

I was still in my suit and tie because I was too depressed to shower. I'd probably stay exactly like that until I had to go to court in the morning. Of course, I would change my suit. But I probably wouldn't shower.

I sat up and rubbed my throbbing temple, feeling inexplicable pain emerge in the strangest places. Heartbreak was more unbearable than any physical damage I'd ever received. There were no antibiotics that could cure the infection.

I'd just have to deal with it.

I stared at my phone even though Rose's name wouldn't appear on the screen. Sometimes I pictured my phone lighting up with a text message, her name sitting right above it.

But it remained black.

Minutes passed before someone came into my mind. She was from my past, but her face comforted me. Even though our relationship didn't work out, we were friends before we were lovers. For some reason I wanted to talk to her.

Or maybe I was just desperate.

I called her and didn't expect her to answer. The last time I called her was over a year ago. She probably didn't even have the same number anymore. I listened to it ring, wondering if a stranger would answer the call.

"Hello?" Francesca's soft voice came over the line. "Kyle?"

"Hey…I hope this isn't a bad time." I couldn't force myself to sound remotely happy. It was impossible.

"Of course not. Are you alright?"

"Uh…no." Despite our time apart she still knew me well. We did spend a year together. No matter how much things had changed, we couldn't change the past. "I'm pretty low, honestly."

"I'm so sorry. Talk to me." A baby cried in the background. "Shh, baby," she said gently.

I forgot about her pregnancy. Her daughter must be a few months old. "How's Suzie?"

"Fussy. She gets upset if I stop paying attention to her for just a second."

"Just like her father," I teased.

"How about you come by and see her?"

Being anywhere besides my apartment sounded fantastic. "If that's okay."

"Of course it is. Let me give you my address."

***

They had a house just outside the city in Connecticut. It was two stories, white and beautiful. A large yard was in the front with crisp, green grass. And the backyard was blocked off by an elegant white fence.

It was perfect for her.

I knocked on the door and immediately heard a baby cry.

"I'll be right back, sweetheart." Francesca's voice trailed from the other side of the house. A moment later, she opened the door. She wore a loose dress with her hair pulled into a braid over one shoulder. She was still carrying some baby weight but you could hardly tell. "Hey." She gave me a genuine smile before she invited me inside.

I took a look around, marveling at the hardwood floors and elegant furniture. "Your place reminds me of the shop."

"I'm always cooking so it's fitting." She guided me into the living room where Suzie lay in the playpen. She stopped crying once we walked into the room. With blue eyes exactly identical to Hawke's, she looked up at me. I didn't care for babies and never thought they were cute—but this one was special. "Wow...she's beautiful."

"Thank you." She grabbed Suzie and cradled her in her arms.

I sat beside her and watched her rock her child. "She looks just like you—except the eyes."

"I know," she said fondly. "She couldn't be more perfect."

Suzie stared at me the entire time, fascinated.

"Would you like to hold her?"

"Sure." I carefully took her from her hands and held her on my lap. She was lighter than I expected her to be. "How's motherhood?"

"So wonderful," she said with a happy sigh. "There's nothing like it."

I gently rocked Suzie back and forth and admired her beauty. Her skin was vibrant just the way Francesca's was. And she had the same dark hair. "I'm happy for you."

"I'm happy for me too. And Hawke is already wrapped around her finger."

"I can imagine." I gently handed her back.

Sunday

Francesca took her then wrapped her in a thin blanket. "So, what's on your mind, Kyle? On the phone you sounded...devastated."

Suzie lit up my life for just a moment, and I forgot about my pain. But then it came rushing back to me in a crushing wave. "There was this woman I was seeing...but we aren't seeing each other anymore."

With Suzie secured in her arms, she watched me with a sad look. The sincerity was in her eyes, that she wanted me to be happy. "I'm so sorry, Kyle."

"Thanks..."

"What happened?"

I told her the entire story, from the very beginning to the very end.

Francesca was speechless, unable to process the trauma Rose went through. "Oh my god..."

"I understand why this relationship will never work. I know where she's coming from. But I can't let her go. It's too hard."

Francesca held Suzie tighter.

jealous of me, but after Francesca married him he didn't seem threatened by anything.

Francesca turned back to me, the happiness on her face dissipating when she remembered the content of our conversation.

"I'm so jealous of you." The words left my lips on their own. I shouldn't have said them, but it was already done by the time I realized my mistake.

Hawke looked up, taking his eyes off his daughter.

"Kyle, you'll get her back." She patted my hand.

"No, I won't," I said miserably. "I screwed it up. I should have told her beforehand. It's my fault."

"It was a difficult situation. No matter what you did, it was risky."

I wished Rose saw it that way. "I don't know what to do. I've given her space for the past week in the hope that was all she needed but I haven't heard from her."

Hawke rocked the chair slightly backward and forward, his daughter laying on one of his large forearms. "I think I walked in at the wrong time..."

"Kyle is having relationship problems," Francesca explained.

"Yeah, I don't have one," I said bitterly. "I find this amazing woman, and I lose her..."

Hawke didn't look at me the way he used to. It was like we never knew each other prior to his marriage to Francesca. He didn't see me as someone who slept with his wife before he married her. "Then get her back." He said it simply, like it was the easiest thing in the world to accomplish.

I shook my head. "It's more complicated than that."

"Is it more complicated than searching the world and trying to fall in love again?" The look in his eyes was victorious, like he knew he had me. "You only have one great love in your life. If she was it, then you can't give up. It's as simple as that."

He walked away from the love of his life twice— but he always came back. Now he was there to stay. "You left Francesca. In this scenario, she left me. If someone wants to break up, you break up."

"Does she love you?" Hawke asked.

Even if she never told me I would have known. "Yeah."

"Then what she says is irrelevant. Be there for her like you never were apart. Be her boyfriend without permission. She's stuck with you and make her accept it." Hawke pulled the blanket over Suzie's shoulder, keeping her warm.

That might work on another woman, but it wouldn't work on her. "She's sensitive to stuff like that..."

"Maybe to other people," he said. "But not to you."

Francesca cleared her throat. "Hawke, Rose has been through some hard times..." She didn't give away her secret, but the look in her eyes said enough.

"It doesn't change anything," Hawke said. "Love is a battlefield. And this is a war you can't afford to lose."

"When did he become so poetic?" I whispered to Francesca.

Her eyes lit up with warmth. "He's always been poetic—he just doesn't show it to anyone but me."

"Lucky me," I said with a chuckle.

"Do you want this?" He leaned forward with Suzie still tucked safely in his arm. "Do you want what Francesca and I have?"

More than anything. Now that I'd had a taste of it I realized how amazing it was. Just sitting on the couch and watching TV with Rose was an adventure. I didn't want to take that journey with anyone else. "I do."

"Then figure it out," he said. "Have Frankie talk to her. She's good at this sort of thing."

I released a sarcastic laugh. "I doubt Rose wants to hear from my ex-girlfriend."

"She's not your ex-girlfriend." Hawke said it with such confidence it was almost believable. "The moment you meet your soul mate all the women before that no longer exist. It's like they never happened."

I knew what he meant.

"She has no reason to be jealous. Just like I have no reason to be jealous of you."

"Awe…" Francesca leaned toward him and gave him a kiss.

Did marriage change him that much? He was almost a completely different person. Would it change me too?

Hawke rubbed his nose against hers before he pulled away. "I'm going to put Suzie to bed." He rose to his feet, his daughter cradled to his chest. "I'll see you later, Kyle. Hope you take my advice." He walked down the hallway and disappeared into one of the bedrooms.

"Wow," I said. "He's a new man."

She smiled proudly. "I think being married gives him an new outlook on life."

"I'll say."

"And being a father has matured him by decades."

"In a good way?"

She stared at her fingers before she looked at me again. "He had a troubled childhood growing up. When he got older, things weren't easy either. He takes his responsibility as a father much differently than the rest of us do. I think that's why he's so different. The moment she was born, he was a new man."

"That's sweet."

"He's a very sweet man."

Their happiness kept reminding me of my misery. I couldn't get it out of my head.

Francesca read my mind. "You remember my relationship with Hawke. It was rocky and difficult, to say the least."

I nodded in agreement.

"Not all romances are easy and carefree. Our relationship was difficult, and Axel's relationship with Marie had some dark times too."

"What's your point?"

"That this isn't the end—just a dark time."

CHAPTER THREE

Sick

Rose

I spent my time cooped up in my apartment.

I didn't go to the office, choosing to work from home. I didn't take on any new clients, and whenever they called, I let it go to voicemail. My broken heart inhibited me from doing anything besides sulk.

Kyle was still in my heart, taking up all the space that remained. He charmed me months ago, his persuasion undeniable. When I went to sleep every night I saw his face in my dreams—and my nightmares.

I couldn't swallow the betrayal. It marked my skin permanently, acting as a tattoo I could never remove.

Since he knew nearly the entire time, I reexamined the pivotal points in our relationship. Were those moments real? Or was he just thinking about the terrible things that happened to me?

It was my privacy that had been abused, and it was even worse when he didn't tell me the information he had. He saw a different image of me, one that I didn't want anyone else to see.

But he did.

Now I remembered our first kiss in a different way. I thought he was taking it slow because I was cautious. I thought he didn't want to rush into anything because he wanted to cultivate a relationship with me.

But now I knew the truth.

He saw me as a rape victim, and he trekked gently.

When we first made love, I thought all he saw was me. He didn't see the past because he didn't know about it. He didn't think of the terrible things that I experienced. All he saw was me.

But that wasn't the case.

How could I continue on in a relationship when he was preparing for the trial to put my rapist in jail? How could he work on that all day and want to spend time with me afterward? How could he take on the case without telling me about it?

What else was he keeping from me?

Could I trust him with anything?

Now I knew he was too good to be true. There was no way a beautiful man like that could want a woman like me. He had a sick fascination with weak women, ones that had been broken. Maybe he was just sensitive because of what happened to his sister, but I felt like there was something else going on.

How could he want me after I was tainted?

It simply wasn't possible.

Kyle didn't call me over the next week. He left me in peace, something I appreciated. When he broke into my apartment and lurked until I arrived, it terrified me. Now that I saw him in a new light, I was a little scared of him. He would never hurt me, but my heart still exploded with warning.

Hopefully, he would let me go. I said we were done, and we needed to go our separate ways. When he walked out of my apartment, he seemed to accept that.

It was hard to picture myself moving on from this. In a few months I'd start dating again, trying to find someone to spend my life with. But would I ever find anyone? Kyle was the only man I cared about, but he ended up being a liar. Now I lost all hope of ever finding anyone else.

There was no one else.

***

I started jogging again. I did my usual route through the park. I started running longer distances to purposely exhaust myself so I could fall asleep at bedtime. If not, I would toss and turn all night.

I'd gotten used to sleeping with Kyle. His warm body kept me warm during the night, and even the irritating things he did were something I missed. Sometimes he snored, and I would kick him gently so he would stop. Sometimes he would hug the covers and even some of the pillows.

I missed all of that.

The week dragged on slowly until I finally reached the two-week mark. It'd been two weeks since I'd last seen or spoken to Kyle.

But it felt like an eternity.

I hadn't been following up with the trial because I wasn't sure if I wanted to know how it was proceeding. If Peter got away with it again, I'd definitely lose sleep. Knowing he was out there and possibly doing the same thing he did to both Audrey and I would be sickening.

And I didn't want to hear anything about Kyle.

I continued to exist in my tiny bubble of life. I stayed in my apartment and only left for groceries and exercise. The little things I used to enjoy, like basketball, haunted me. I couldn't watch a game without thinking about him. And I couldn't watch my favorite show either.

Everything haunted me.

How many weeks would I have to wait until this pain went away? How many months? Would it take years?

I wished I had that answer.

Sunday

***

I lay in bed and stared at the ceiling. It was 2:15 a.m.

I wasn't sure why I bothered putting myself to bed when I never got any rest. This mattress was suddenly the most uncomfortable thing in the world. The sheets were itchy and old, and even my clothes didn't fit right.

My phone started to ring on the nightstand. The sound pierced the silence of my bedroom, echoing off the four walls.

I immediately snatched it and hoped it would be Kyle. I'd been staring at my phone every day for weeks expecting his name to appear on the screen. A part of me wanted him to leave me alone, to give me space so I could get over him.

But the bigger part of me, the pathetic one, hoped this phone call would happen.

I cleared my throat before I answered. But there wasn't much point in doing that since I didn't speak. I listened to the silence on the other line, trying to hear him breathe or move.

"Hey." His desolated tone was unmistakable.

"Hey…"

He fell silent, the quietness doing all the talking for us. His gentle breathing hit the receiver from time-to-time, and once in a while he released a deep sigh that released louder than he meant to.

I wondered if he could hear my rapid breathing and understand how nervous I was.

"The jurors are deliberating."

Is that the only reason why he called? To give me an update on the trial? The disappointment hit me harder than I expected it to. "Oh…"

"They started yesterday but were unable to reach a verdict."

Was that bad? Was that good?

"I'm scared." His voice cracked in a way it never had before. "If they have to deliberate that means it could go either way. I really thought they would immediately assume he was guilty. I did everything right…put the evidence on a silver platter."

"They'll find him guilty."

"What's with this guy?" His voice blew up immediately. "Is it because he's easy on the eyes? Does it make him less of a threat? The world ticks me off. People tick me off."

It was important to me that Peter was found guilty. But now I was starting to think it was more important to him. "No matter what the vote is, you did your best. That's all that matters."

"No, that's not all that matters," he snapped. "If he walks, every woman in Manhattan is at risk. I can't let this guy go free. If he does, I'll murder him myself. I'll track him down and shoot him in an alleyway."

While I believed his rage, I didn't believe his hatred. "No, you won't."

"You don't know me very well."

"I wouldn't want you to. So let's stop talking about it."

"It doesn't matter what you want," he snapped. "What I want matters. And I want him dead or behind bars. It's one or the other."

"Let's see what the jury decides and we'll go from there." I needed to say something to keep him calm.

"If I lose this case, I'll never forgive myself. Not ever."

"Don't be so hard on yourself," I whispered. "There are many other factors in play here."

"That doesn't matter. I promised myself I would win this case. I promised I would get you the justice both of you deserve."

"You will, Kyle."

A frustrated sigh escaped his lips then he fell silent on the phone. He didn't speak for minutes, his rage slowly dissipating over the phone line. Somehow, I could feel it drifting away. "God, I miss you."

My chest immediately tensed.

"I can't sleep. I can't think. I can't eat. Shit, I can't do anything."

Those words were both beautiful and painful. This time apart was a lot harder than I expected it to be. He was constantly on my mind, and I found myself wondering what he was doing rather than focusing on my work.

"It's been hard. I feel like I don't know who I am anymore."

Listening to him was unbearable.

"Sweetheart?"

Hearing that nickname caused the tears to form deep in my throat. I missed hearing that name play on my ears. I missed hearing it every time he greeted me and every time he said goodbye. "I'm here."

"I'm sorry if I'm bothering you. I just couldn't sleep, and I wanted to talk to you..."

"You aren't bothering me." I regretted saying that the moment it left my mouth. I needed to control myself and stay strong. I broke up with him for a reason, and that reason hadn't changed.

"I can't sleep. Can you?"

I haven't slept in two weeks. "Not really."

"I've been living off caffeine and other forms of caffeine. It keeps me going...but I know I'm going to crash and burn really soon."

"I haven't been living off caffeine…" I haven't been living at all.

He fell quiet again, listening to the static over the phone. "What have you been up to?"

"Just work. Jogging." Absolutely nothing.

"Cool…"

I didn't want him to get off the phone. Listening to his voice was actually making me tired. The stress left my body, and I felt at peace. He wasn't beside me, but hearing his breathing made it seem like he was there—with me.

"I'll let you go." The depression was heavy in his voice, like he'd never be happy again.

"Can you stay on the line?" I said it without thinking, my heart making all the big decisions at the moment.

"Sure."

I turned on my side and kept the phone pressed to my ear. Even when he didn't say anything, just knowing he was there comforted me. I moved the pillow so it felt like he was beside me. Then I closed my eyes, feeling myself drift.

"Good night, sweetheart."

***

All I could think about was the trial.

The jury may have come to their decision, and they would announce it at any moment. I wanted justice for what was done to me, and Audrey deserved the same. But I also wanted Kyle to receive the satisfaction he desperately deserved. He worked night and day on this case, and he needed a guilty verdict as much as I did.

He never mentioned my case, and when he did speak of it he was always restrained. He never put the topic directly in his mind because he couldn't focus all of his thoughts on it—because it was too difficult. He was invested in this just as much as I was, and if he didn't get the conviction he'd never sleep well again.

I should be there for him.

He worked his ass off for me. This case wasn't even his to begin with, but he took it because he believed no one else would put in as much effort. The gesture was beautiful and heartfelt—even if he kept it a secret for so long.

I went to the courthouse with a heavy heart. If Peter walked out of there, I wasn't sure if I could handle it. But I felt like I should be there anyway. I walked into the courtroom then slowly moved down the aisles. People were whispering among themselves and the jury was still deliberating.

I stood a seat in the front row, directly behind Kyle and Audrey.

Kyle remained upright in his chair, holding himself perfectly straight with powerful shoulders. He didn't hint at the stress swirling inside his body. He remained strong for his client, who looked like a mess beside him.

I stared at the back of his head, wanting him to know I was there. But I wasn't sure how to get his attention without causing a distraction to everyone else.

Kyle tensed slightly, like the temperature changed and made him feel cool. Then, like he knew I was there all along, he turned around in the chair to look at me. Somehow, he sensed I was behind him. Perhaps he got a scent of my perfume or felt the change in the air. Whatever it was, he picked up on it.

He stared at me with his pragmatic eyes, showing the fierce and unforgiving prosecutor he was at the moment. But deep down inside, I could see the Kyle I knew so well. He was in there, terrified.

He left his chair then approached the fence that separated his seat from the rest of the courtroom.

I stood up and did the same, feeling my hands move to the beam. My body automatically wanted to hug him, to comfort him in some way.

"Still waiting," he whispered.

"It'll be okay, Kyle."

He bowed his head then rubbed the back of his neck. "I hope so. I want this so much...it hurts."

I automatically grabbed his hand and held it within my own.

He stared down at our joined affection, the hope coming into his eyes.

"I'm here for you."

He squeezed my fingers. "Thanks for coming. I could feel you behind me...I suddenly felt a little better."

I wanted to hold him in my arms and never let go.

The jury filed in from their deliberation room, taking their seats.

Kyle eyed them before he turned back to me. "It's time."

My body ached to comfort his, and I wanted to make this better. He was invested in this case, probably more invested than any other case he'd worked on. I appreciated everything he did, even if he didn't get the conviction. I rose on my tiptoes and gave him a quick kiss on the lips.

He flinched at the touch initially, but then he kissed me back.

I pulled away and felt my cheeks blush in embarrassment. My actions were automatic, and I should have controlled myself better.

He didn't smile with his lips but he smiled with his eyes.

I sat down and bunched my hands together in my lap, prepared for the worst.

Kyle adjusted his tie then took a seat. His massive back was in my view, and it looked like the side of a mountain. His breathing was deep and even, controlled and slow.

Everyone was dead silent, waiting to hear the decision.

The first jury member stood and handed the note to the bailiff, who handed it to the judge. The judge opened the paper and read the decision.

I eyed Peter, hoping he was scared shitless at that very moment. If he were convicted, he'd spend the rest of his life behind bars. He might be able to get out early on parole, but that still wouldn't be for at least twenty years.

A lot could happen in twenty years.

The judge cleared his throat before he spoke. "Peter Gamble, based on the charges of rape, sex trafficking, and assault, a jury of your peers has condemned you—guilty."

Kyle didn't react at all, his body not moving an inch. He didn't even flinch.

Audrey covered her mouth and gasped, tears springing into her eyes.

Peter retained the same indifferent look. It was like he hadn't heard the judge's pronouncement at all.

"You're sentenced to life in prison without parole." The judge struck his mallet. "This meeting is adjourned."

Instead of turning to me, Kyle moved his focus to Audrey. He placed his hand on her shoulder, comforting her silently.

She cried into her hands, sobbing.

"He can't hurt you again, Audrey," he said gently.

"Thank you so much." She wiped her tears away and tried to remain calm. "I couldn't have gotten through this without you."

He pulled her in for a hug and allowed her to weep against his chest. The emotions were hitting her all at once, shaking the ground she stood on. Her hair obscured her face, giving her the privilege of crying without being seen.

Kyle rubbed her back gently while his chin rested on her head. He was patient, giving her everything she needed in that moment.

After several moments she pulled way. "I'm sorry...I got make up on your jacket."

"It's okay. That's what dry-cleaning is for." He gave her a friendly smile. "Now that this is over you should go home and get some rest. You can sleep easy tonight."

"You're right..." She gathered her purse and gave him a final look. "I'll never thank you enough for your kindness."

"I'm just doing my job."

She wiped her eyes before she walked out of the courtroom. Peter was being escorted through the side door in police custody. His parents sat in the front row, and his mom cried into a tissue. I wasn't sure if she was crying because she was disappointed in her son. Or if it was because she thought he was innocent.

Kyle rose to his feet and gathered his papers. He shoved everything inside his satchel then pulled it over his shoulder. His eyes drifted to Peter just as he walked out and disappeared altogether.

I approached the table, my hand resting on the corner.

When he looked at me the relief was in his eyes. Now he could get some sleep tonight knowing he won the trial. Peter was off the streets, and now there wouldn't be any more victims at his hands. He took a deep breath that showed just how exhausted he was. "I feel like a weight has been lifted off me…"

"You did an amazing job, Kyle."

"Seeing Audrey finally breathe easy…made everything worthwhile."

He was the most compassionate man in the world. I'd never seen anyone expend so much effort for someone he hardly knew. "You're a hero."

"And getting justice for what he did to you, even if it was four years too late, heals me a little bit. I know it can't erase the past. I know it can't undo the things that have already been done. But…I hope it helps."

"It does."

"Good. I'm glad." He looked at me with a mixture of affection and longing. "He deserves to pay for what he's done, and not just to you. I'm sure there are so many other women out there who never spoke up."

"I know..." It was terrible to think about.

He put his hands in his pockets as everyone filed out of the courtroom. The judge gathered his papers and left, still wearing his long, black robes. The jury disappeared through their private exit. His eyes remained glued to mine. "Since I won the case, can I have something?"

He could have anything he wanted. "What is it?"

"I haven't slept in weeks. And I'd do anything to finally rest." His insomnia didn't step from the trial and all the stress that came with it. It came from the loss of me—his empty bed.

I got decent sleep the night before because he called. But if he hadn't, I probably would have been up all night as well. Getting back together wasn't an option but I didn't want to push him away. After everything we'd both been through we needed some comfort. "Your place or mine?"

***

Kyle passed his living room and kitchen and immediately headed straight for the bedroom. He didn't even bothering turning on the lights. Once he was inside, he stripped off his suit and tossed it on the ground. His shoes and socks were gone, and all that was left was his boxers.

I suddenly felt self-conscious getting naked in front of him. That would give him the wrong message, and I didn't want this sleepover to lead to something else.

Without asking me about it, Kyle detected my worry. He pulled a t-shirt and a pair of shorts from his drawer then tossed it at me. "They're big—but clean."

I held them in my hands immediately noticed the smell. They felt clean like they just came out of the dryer. The fabric softener entered my nose, but I also detected his natural scent. I didn't realize I could be so excited just to smell him.

Kyle got under the covers and lay on his back, his eyes already closed. The curtain over his window was drawn shut, and visibility was poor in his room. Instead of bothering with the bathroom I just changed where I was.

Kyle didn't open his eyes once.

When I was finished I got into bed beside him. The second I felt the sheets and the warmth, I realized how much I missed his mattress. It was softer than mine and bigger too. I had a queen size bed whereas he had a king. But I guess it didn't matter since we were usually wrapped up in each other anyway.

Kyle didn't open his eyes, but his arms reached out and snagged me like a fish on a hook-line. He pulled me across the sheets until I was pressed tightly into his side, his hard chest acted as an anchor. One arm was wrapped around my shoulders and his hand was inserted into my hair. A quiet sigh escaped his lips, one full of peace and exhaustion. "This feels so good. I forgot, actually."

When I listened to his breathing over the phone, it was enough to make it seem like he was really there. But feeling him in real life was so much better. I could feel his strong heart beating under my fingertips. I could feel his breathing become slower and slower with every passing minute. And I could feel him sleep away into a land of dreams.

***

When I woke up the following morning, Kyle was gone. He'd vacated the bed sometime earlier since his side of the bed was cold. The sheets were lifeless, like he took all the energy with him.

I sat up in alarm because waking up to his absence was actually painful. Without him there, I was just alone. I'd gotten a great night of sleep but had an uncomfortable waking. "Kyle?"

The bedroom door was shut, and when I blinked the sleep from my eyes I realized the noticed the sound of moving pots in the kitchen. I slivered out of bed and walked out.

Kyle flipped a pancake high into the air and caught it with the pan. The concentration on his face made it look like he was playing a game with himself. He ground his teeth together slightly until the pancake was safe in the pan.

"Are you going to go for the gold?"

He flinched when he realized he'd been spotted. "Maybe I will. I think I have what it takes."

I'd rolled his boxers five times so they would fit around my waist. The shirt reached to the area just below my knees. I was being swallowed up into a sea of clothes. "It smells good in here."

"Because I'm making breakfast." He slid the pancake onto a plate before he turned the pan to the stove. "Hope you're hungry."

"I'm always conveniently hungry when food is around."

He chuckled then handed me a plate. "Well, I hope you're conveniently hungry for eggs, bacon, and pancakes."

"I am, actually."

He set the plates on the table then took a seat. "Coffee is okay?" The mugs were already sitting there.

"They are perfect." I sat down and ate beside him, feeling the crunch of the bacon between my teeth. "What made you decide to make breakfast?"

He shrugged. "I woke up in a good mood."

"I'm glad I get to benefit from it."

"I haven't slept like that in weeks. When I opened my eyes today I could actually think clearly. Everything has been a blur lately, the trial...us." His eyes were glued to his plate.

My life had been a blur too. I didn't know what to say to his comment so I held my silence. In our time apart, I'd been doing a good job of steering clear of him. But when he called, I broke down. "I know."

"I've suffered a lot in my life, but that was a new level of pain." He held his fork without taking a bite. "When Francesca left, I was devastated. It was difficult to get on with my life. But these past two weeks have been so much worse than that...by a landslide."

I eyed the steam erupting from my coffee, drifting high to the ceiling. The silence of the apartment was even more deafening now that Kyle had stopped talking. Moments like this made me care about the past. Maybe he knew the truth of what happened to me and didn't tell me even after we slept together, but he was a good man.

I could forgive him, right?

Kyle set down his fork then turned his gaze on me. "With everything that's happened between us, can't we just move on? Can we forget about the past? We love each other and that's all that matters."

I wanted to say yes because my heart was still painfully attached to him. I wanted to sleep with him every night and kiss him before he left for work. But then I remembered our relationship. That entire time I was learning to trust him, and he knew everything about me when I wasn't ready to reveal it. That changed everything. It made me feel naïve.

"Sweetheart, I know it's hard. But you can give me another chance, right?"

I wanted to. "It's different..."

"What is?"

"Our relationship. Everything that happened between us is void—because it was all a lie."

"That's not true."

"But it is. Now I don't know what was real and what wasn't real. When you said things to me, were they genuine? Or were you just staying that because you knew what happened to me? How can I ever tell?"

He stared at the table while he compiled his answer. When he was ready he turned back to me. "I guess I did say and do certain things when I knew the truth. But it was never to manipulate you. It was always to help you."

"But how could you want me anyway?" My deepest fears were coming to the surface. "How could any man want me after what happened? You read my file. You know exactly what they did to me..." That night still tarnished me, but I did feel a little better knowing Peter was in jail. But the rest of them got away.

"Because I don't think about it. And when I do think about it, it doesn't change the way I look at you. You were a victim in all of that, and it's wrong for anyone to hold that against you. You aren't damaged goods. You aren't broken. You aren't impure. You're just as beautiful and whole as you were before it happened."

I lowered my gaze when I listened to all those sweet things.

"If you gave me a chance, we could really move on. You could learn to forget about the past and look at yourself in a different way. You and I could have an intense physical relationship that would make you feel amazing things. But you have to give me another chance."

Despite everything he said, I just couldn't do it. "I don't think we can just pick up where we left off."

He quickly turned away, like he didn't want me to see his expression. "What if we started a new relationship? Started over?"

"Can we start over?" I asked. "Is that possible after everything that's come to pass?"

"I think so—if we want it enough."

Would I ever be able to look at him in a different way? He had sex with me without telling me what he knew. If I'd known, it would have changed the events of that night. I certainly wouldn't have been ready. And that made me extremely uncomfortable. "I'm sorry, Kyle."

He pushed his plate away, a disappointed sigh escaping his lips. "If you need more time, I'll give it to you. But don't end us forever."

"It's not about time…"

"Then what will you do?" he asked. "Be alone then start dating again? See them for a while and then tell them what happened? With me, you don't need to tell me anything. I know exactly what you went through because my sister went through the same thing. And I don't judge you for it." He couldn't hold back his frustration. It was starting to seep into his voice.

"I don't know what the future holds because I'm not that far ahead…but I know I shouldn't stay here out of fear."

He released another deep sigh, like he was holding back whatever he wanted to say. "I think you're being unfair."

"I think you should have told me the truth the second you found out." We could point the finger at each other all day long, but it wouldn't get us anywhere.

"You didn't tell me either so stop blaming me."

"It's my business, and I have the right to keep it a secret. But for you to know, to prosecute my tormentor, go through all my personal files and know every little detail that happened that night, and not breathe a single word of it to me, is wrong. You had an advantage in this relationship and you exploited it every chance you got. You played a game that was rigged from the beginning. Don't downplay your actions, Kyle. They would make anyone upset."

He rested his elbows on the table and looked into the living room. His side profile was immobile, not showing a single sign or feeling. But he suddenly felt cold, the air around him dropping a few degrees. "You're exaggerating. I didn't exploit you."

"It felt like it."

He rose to his feet, pushing his chair back with his knees. "I took that case because I didn't trust anyone else to win. I took it because I wanted to put that asshole behind bars so you would have some peace. I did all of that for you. If that doesn't prove my love, I don't know what does." He grabbed his keys and wallet off the counter. "I was patient with you, understanding. I helped you overcome your fears. I bent backwards trying to get you to trust me. But if you just see me as a monster, then why am I even bothering?" He stopped in front of the door and stared me down, the fury burning deep in his eyes. "Good bye, Rose." He walked out and slammed the door behind him. It was his apartment but he left just to get away from me.

I remained at the kitchen table and played his final words in my head. The pain seeped into the air and dissolved into my skin. He had every right to be angry, to be upset.

But so did I.

Sunday

CHAPTER FOUR

Fury

Kyle

Now I was just angry.

Rose saw the world in black and white. According to her, my actions were terrible and unforgivable. But to an objective person, it was clear there was no right or wrong answer to the situation. If I had told her what I knew, what would that have achieved? It would have just pushed her away. If I told her when she declared her love for me that would have ruined the moment. And since she said those sweet words to me, what did it matter what I knew or didn't know?

On top of that, I took her case to bring him down. I didn't do it for the paycheck. I did it because I was the only person I trusted to do the job right. There was too much on the line for anything to go haywire. Rose's justice was at stake, and I wasn't letting anyone take that away from her.

But that wasn't good enough for her.

Underneath all my anger was the pain of losing her. It festered deep down below, invading every crevasse and vein. But the fury was at the forefront, driving me insane with rage.

I couldn't believe she left me.

Days went by and I still didn't feel better. I began to resent her, to feel so much anger I couldn't take it anymore. While most people would just feel sad and hopeless, I took a different route.

I walked into The Muffin Girl because I needed to let out some steam. Even though Francesca married someone else, she still knew me well. She was someone I could talk to, even after all this time. She may be at home taking care of her daughter, but she might be back at work as well.

I suspected it was the latter.

Francesca couldn't stay away from her kitchens very long.

I walked into the back like I knew where I was going, and no one paid any attention to me. It'd been over a year since I'd been inside her bakery. It was exactly as I remembered it. The bags of flour still sat on the top shelf, and the place was packed with a line that never seemed to go down.

I headed into the cake kitchen and saw Francesca working on a creation. It was a three-tier cake, white and pristine. She was creating sugar seashells along the sides. Her baby weight had gone done considerably and she was almost back to where she used to be.

"Hey, are you busy?"

She stopped what she was doing and turned to me. "Oh hey. I didn't see you there."

"It's okay. I kind of snuck up on you."

She set down her decorating tools then washed her hands in the sink. They were covered in frosting and sugar.

I eyed the cake, impressed with her handiwork. "You really are talented."

"Thank you." She patted her hands dry then returned to me. "I suspect your presence means it didn't work out with Rose?"

I shrugged with a sad look.

"I'm sorry, Kyle."

"Where's Suzie?" I changed the subject because the strong sense of sadness washed over me.

"She's staying with her Aunt Marie today."

"Oh, she must be having fun."

"She's got two cousins to play with."

"Really?" I asked in surprise. "Axel and Marie already have two kids?" How was that possible?

"Twins." She answered the question on my face. "Twin boys."

"Oh, good for them."

"They're very happy. And I'm happy that Marie is a housewife now so she can watch my daughter for free." She began to glow when she mentioned her daughter, like she missed her immensely.

"Free childcare. Nothing beats that."

"It's true," she said with a laugh.

"I'm surprised you're back at work so soon."

"Suzie is three months old." She undid the flowery apron around her waist and set it on the table. "I had to go back to work sometime."

"But you own this place. You can do whatever you want."

"Not when I have wedding cakes to create."

"You still haven't found anyone?"

She shook her head. "Strange, huh? Wedding cakes are pretty stressful. If it's not absolutely perfect, a bride may murder you. Very few people want to take that on."

"I can imagine..."

She pulled out two chairs and took a seat in one. "What's up, Kyle?"

I fell into the chair next to her and sighed. "I think Rose and I are finished."

"Tell me what happened." Her entire focus was glued to me, the sympathy written all over her face.

"I won the trial."

"Isn't that good news?"

"It is. Now he's going to jail for life—without parole."

"And that's exactly what he deserves."

"I got Rose justice, along with Audrey. Now both of them will be able to sleep better at night. Rose and I got closer that night. She slept over and was there the next morning."

"Did you sleep together?"

"No. Just cuddled."

"Then what happened?"

"She said she couldn't trust me anymore. She said it changes everything..."

Francesca gave me a heartfelt look. "Because you didn't tell her when you found out the truth?"

I nodded. "She said she wouldn't have slept with me if she'd known. So, I manipulated her into doing something she wouldn't have done otherwise."

"This is complicated," she said with a sigh. "Her reasoning isn't logical, but neither one of us can begin to understand what she's feeling. Traumas like that really change people. She's unable to trust anyone, even people who deserve it. To her, this decision makes the most sense."

"But it doesn't," I argued. "We love each other and that's all that matters."

"Maybe things would have been different if you weren't the lawyer on the trial. In that situation, you had access to intricate details, stuff she'd probably want to hide from the man she's seeing."

"But I did that for her. I didn't trust anyone else to win the case."

"I'm sure she understands that, but it doesn't erase the shock of the whole situation."

"I apologized to her." The frustration was starting to eat me alive. "I said I was sorry. I told her I loved her. What more could I possibly do?"

She bowed her head.

"I don't want to lose her. But...she's really making me angry."

"Kyle, you were patient with her for three months. Be patient a little longer."

"Be patient for what?" I snapped.

"Be patient because you want to be with her. Unless that's changed..."

I was still livid—but I knew how I felt underneath. "No, it hasn't."

"Then give her some space."

"How much space? How long?"

"Until she realizes she can't live without you."

Would that day ever come? Would she even notice she felt that way if it smacked her right in the forehead?

"When Hawke pushed me away, I always knew he would come back—every time."

"Then why did you date me?"

"Because I never planned on taking him back."

We know how that worked out.

"Did you tell Rose how you feel?"

I knew what she was referring to. "No."

"Why not? That could make a huge difference."

"I can't even convince her to give me another chance. You think I'm going to convince her that she's my soul mate?" That was a long shot—a very long shot.

"Maybe not right this second. But you will."

I didn't see how I would manage that.

"You need to get her in the same room as you. Spend time with her without bringing up your relationship at all."

"Why?"

"When Hawke and I spent a lot of time together for Marie and Axel's wedding, there was no escape from each other. We were basically locked in a room together with no escape. That's when things really started happening."

"Well, I can't lock her in a room—especially with her past."

"But there has to be some way for you to spend time with her."

"I can't think of anything. She was designing my beach house but that went to shit. There's no way she would take up the project again."

Francesca fell quiet. She stared at me, but her eyes were seeing something besides my face. "Hawke is about to move his business to a new place. It's expanding, and he needs something bigger and grander."

"Good for him…"

"What if he hires her to take care of it? After the contract is signed, you'll take over as his lawyer or something. Hawke will tell you what he wants and you'll relay that information."

"That sounds far-fetched."

"It's not ideal but it should work. It's a long project with a lot of hours. And by the time she figures out who she'll be dealing with it'll be too late."

I still wasn't convinced this was the best course of action. "She'll know I set everything up."

"Not really. Hawke is your client and you can't control what he does."

There was another problem in this plan. "Why would Hawke help me? He doesn't owe me anything."

"Of course he'll help you."

Not after I slept with her.

"He wants the best for you," she said. "You heard what he said at the house."

"But his interaction with me was limited. If we do this, he'll be directly spending time with me."

She shook her head. "I admit Hawke was very rough around the edges a year ago but he's different now. Honestly."

I still wasn't sure if this was a good idea—no matter how much I wanted Rose.

The sound of heavy footsteps approached, and we both looked up to see Hawke enter the kitchen. He wore a suit that reeked of expense, and the watch on his wrist looked more expensive than a car. His black wedding ring suited his exterior—cold and hard.

This was the second time he walked in on Francesca and I. If I were him, I'd be irritated. I wouldn't want my wife spending time with her ex—no matter what the circumstance was.

After he took me in he walked further into the room, his shiny dress shoes looking brand new. He walked up to Francesca then leaned down to kiss her. The kiss was short but full of longing, like he'd kiss her longer and harder if I weren't around. Without saying a single word he grabbed a chair and pulled it next to Francesca's. He took a seat and rested his hand on her thigh.

He didn't say hello to me but he didn't seem hostile either. He was pretty much indifferent.

Francesca turned back to me. "What do you think?"

"I don't know..."

"I think it's worth the shot," she pressed. "And you lose every shot you don't take."

"You sound like a motivation poster inside a classroom..." Now wasn't the time to make jokes, but my depression was steering the wheel.

"The road to love is never easy," she said. "You should only take it if you really want the reward at the end. If you want Rose, I think you should do this. But if it seems hopeless then you should keep what's left of your heart and move on."

I did want her. Even though she pissed me off like crazy, I still wanted her.

"So, how about it?" Francesca asked.

I turned to Hawke, giving her my answer.

She smiled then turned to him. "We need your help."

"We?" he asked in surprise. "I doubt I can be much help to whatever scheme you've planned."

"Actually, I think you're the perfect person." She grabbed his hand that was resting on her thigh.

"Why do I doubt that?" He turned his gaze on her, and despite his coldness, his look was warm.

"Never doubt me, babe."

He brought her hand to his lips and gently kissed the knuckle. "What do you want me to do?"

Sunday

"It's kind of complicated," Francesca said. "So pay attention."

He squeezed her thigh. "I think I can manage, Muffin."

CHAPTER FIVE

Work

Rose

I went back to the office because it was too difficult to stay home alone. The place no longer had Kyle's smell so it was depressing. I returned to restless nights and lack of sleep.

The office was safe because Kyle had only visited once—when we first started talking. His presence hadn't stained the place and the air was still clean. It was one of the few places I could be without being haunted by his ghost.

The door to the office opened and a tall man walked inside. He was six-two with a powerful body that hinted at his strength. He wore a black suit with a gray tie, looking like a successful executive. His eyes were startling blue, similar to Kyle's. He had dark hair and a light covering of facial hair.

He was good-looking, to say the least.

He wore a black wedding ring on his left hand, and I couldn't help but think how lucky his wife was.

He approached my desk with perfect posture, his eyes glued to my face in an intense way. The moment he walked inside he brought dark clouds with him. The place suddenly became very cold. "Hawke—nice to meet you." He extended his hand.

"Hi..." I shook it then quickly pulled my hand away. "Rose."

He took a seat in the armchair and rested his ankle on the opposite knee. "I'm building a new office just a block over. I have some ideas in mind and I'm looking for an architect to bring my design to life. Are you available?"

Actually, things were pretty slow at the moment. I hadn't been directing much traffic to my business since I'd been under the weather. A lot of things had hit me at once. "I am. But I'd like to understand the scope of the project first."

"Well, it's going to be a third story building. I wanted it designed with elegant architecture—not the modern look. I want beautiful ornate windows along with delicate frescos."

"What kind of business do you run?"

"Investment company."

"I understand." He wanted his business to reek of money, to smell like success. Every person who walked into his office needed to know just how well that business was doing. If they believed in the company, they would throw more money at it.

"So, are you the person for the job?"

"I think so."

"Great." He immediately rose to his feet like he was in a hurry. "My lawyer and I will meet you at the site tomorrow, if you're free."

Why did he need his lawyer present?

"Also…" He pulled out his checkbook and scribbled a number. "Consider this my deposit."

"That's not necessary—"

"I insist." He set the check on the desk. "I want this done as quickly and efficiently as possible. I can't afford any sudden drawbacks." He buttoned the front of his jacket and walked out. "I'll give you the address tomorrow."

"Alright. Thank you."

He waved then disappeared.

That was the easiest job I've ever gotten. Hawke knew exactly what he wanted and knew he wanted me for the job. I wish all my conversations were that simple.

CHAPTER SIX

Showtime

Kyle

I was nervous this would blow up in my face.

Hawke sat beside me in the coffee shop across the street from the lot where the building would go. Hawke already acquired the lot as well as the permission to build, so now he just needed the architect to begin. He sipped his coffee slowly with a bored look on his face.

"I'm not sure if this is a good idea."

"It'll be fine. When she gets here, I'll step out with an important phone call from my wife."

"Even then..."

"I already gave her the deposit. She's stuck."

She could just rip it up.

"And she's already cashed it."

Even then, she could just give it back.

"Pretend you had no idea," Hawke said. "That's not too hard to do."

"Lying isn't too hard to do?" I asked incredulously.

"When the love of your life is on the line, you say and do whatever is necessary to keep her around. So put on your gear and get ready."

"Why are you doing this for me?" He didn't owe me anything, and I almost took Francesca away from him.

He shrugged. "Whatever is important to Francesca is important to me."

"But you're actually letting Rose build your office. That's a big sacrifice."

"All the architects are the same. It's my vision. She's just drawing it out."

"Even then..."

"It sounds like she knows what she's doing. From what I read on her site, she's worked on a significant number of landmarks."

"She has."

"So, I'm sure she's fine." He sipped his coffee again.

I watched him, eyeing the watch on his wrist. "You don't hate me?"

"Why would I hate you?" He pressed his lips tightly together as he rubbed away the coffee stain from his mouth.

"I was with Francesca for nearly a year..." I wasn't just an ex-boyfriend. I was going to marry her at some point. I never received confirmation for it, but I suspected Hawke knew about my proposal. Axel must have told him. Why else would he swoop in and ask Francesca to marry him first?

"I know. And you were good to her. So I have no reason to hate you."

"It's still awkward..."

"Not really," he said. "After we got married our lives started over. It doesn't seem like there was ever anything before us. It's hard to understand, but trust me, you'll get it someday."

Maybe I would. But I probably wouldn't.

"What is it about this woman?"

I shrugged. "What is it about Francesca?"

"Touché." He held up his mug. "She and I are going to start trying again."

"For another baby?" I asked in surprise.

"Yeah. The doctor said everything is ready to go."

"Wow…congratulations." They just had one kid. I couldn't imagine trying to take care of two.

"Thanks. We want them close in age."

"Do you want a boy this time?"

"Actually, no." He said it like the revelation surprised even himself. "Now that I have Suzie, I want another little girl. She's just so cute…and looks just like Francesca."

I smiled. "Suzie does look just like Francesca."

"I wanted to name her Francesca so we could call her Little Frankie but she didn't go for it."

"Suzie Taylor is pretty good."

"Everything goes great with my last name." He gave an arrogant smile.

I eyed the window and waited for her to arrive. A moment later her figure came into the window. She carried her big purse so she could fit her iPad and paperwork inside.

She walked inside and scanned the tables to search for Hawke. When she found him she immediately walked over. It took a moment for her to recognize me, and when she did she stopped in her tracks.

I did my best to look surprised.

She gripped her purse then stared at Hawke with accusation.

"Sorry, do you two know each other?" Hawke asked, eyeing us back and forth.

I kept up my confusion, trying to make it seem as sincere as possible. "Uh...we've worked together before."

Rose took a moment to recover from the shock. I was obviously the last person she expected to see that afternoon.

Hawke eyed her, keeping up with the charade. "Would you like to sit down so we can get to work?"

She eyed the chair before she slowly sat down, her defenses high.

"Kyle is my legal expert on the matter. He's going to be my legal representation for the company." Hawke casually lied out of his ass, doing a remarkable job. "In my line of work, you can never be too careful."

"Business isn't good?" She pulled everything out of her bag and didn't make eye contact with either of us.

I knew the question was meant for me. "He gave me an offer I couldn't refuse."

"I see..." She pulled out all of her supplies then got ready to take notes. "So, let's talk about your plans."

Hawke's phone rang right on cue. "Hey, Muffin. I'm at a meeting right now." He listened to Francesca talk over the phone. "Baby, are you alright? Yeah, I'll be there in a second. Love you." He hung up and rose to his feet. "I'm so sorry, Rose. My wife is at the hospital with our newborn daughter. I have to go."

"Oh..." Rose stiffened in her seat. "Is your daughter okay?"

"I'm not sure," he said. "Something about an infection. But Kyle can take over."

"We can just reschedule," Rose argued. "You have enough on your plate—"

"It's really okay." He patted her shoulder and walked out. "Kyle has my full confidence."

When he was gone she turned back to me, the surprise still heavy in her eyes.

I stared back at her, longing to see her like I never had before. Her auburn brown hair looked softer than usual, and her green eyes were brighter than a lit firework. Those lips were full—ready to be kissed.

God, I missed her.

All the anger burning inside my body disappeared in that moment. Love conquered fury, and I was left with nothing but desperation. Despite my feelings I had to keep it cool. Right now, I was supposed to be astonished she was there.

She gripped her pencil so tightly it might break in half.

I had to remain indifferent, not to mention the relationship at all if I were going to succeed. "Well, shall we begin?"

She clearly wasn't expecting me to say that. "What?"

"With the design? Hawke and I have discussed it extensively and I know exactly what he wants."

She spun the pencil between her fingers, what she usually did when she was thinking. "Did you arrange this?"

"Arrange what, exactly?"

"This." She pointed between us.

I tried to sound as sarcastic as possible. "Yes...I convinced a random guy to pay you to design a building he doesn't even want."

That wiped the suspicion off her face. "Why are you working for him?"

"He offered me a lot of money to do very little."

"But you don't need money."

"But I could use a break from the office." After what I went through with Audrey's trial, no one would question that.

She stopped spinning her pen, convinced.

"I'm sorry this is an awkward situation. I don't want to be here anymore than you do. But we're both adults and we can get this done."

Rose's face suddenly turned pale, as if all the blood shifted to a different part of her body. Her normally beautiful green eyes no longer seemed quite as bright. Her gaze shifted to the table before they returned to my face because she was taken aback by what I said.

If I stopped chasing her, maybe she would come to me.

"You're right…" She opened her notebook and unlocked her iPad.

"Should I sit beside you?" I kept my voice indifferent, like being beside her didn't give me any kind of pleasure whatsoever.

"Yeah, that'd probably be best."

I left the chair then glanced at the counter. "I think I'm going to get a coffee. You want anything?"

"Uh, a blueberry scone please. Thanks."

"You got it." I got in line then ordered my coffee. Then I hovered near the pick-up counter and waited for my name to be called. I busied myself on my phone to keep up my image of indifference.

"Kyle?"

I looked up to see my former secretary. She worked in my office for a few years before she started law school. I hadn't seen her in years. "Hey, long time no see."

She moved into my chest and hugged me with a smile on her face.

I suddenly took advantage of the situation, trying to make Rose jealous. It was an immature thing to do, but I was desperate to get her back. I let the touch linger a little longer than I normally would in the hope Rose would notice. "How's lawyer life treating you?"

"Well, I'm not a lawyer yet." She chuckled and pulled away. She had long blonde hair and typical blue eyes. She would definitely win some cases with looks like that.

"Give it time. And when you are a lawyer, you'll quickly start to hate it." I smiled so she knew I was joking.

"Thanks. What's new with you?"

"You know, just saving the world."

She had a naturally beautiful smile that made it seem like she was happy all the time. "Where's your cape?"

"Stuffed in my back pocket."

The barista called my name and announced my coffee was ready.

"Well, I'll let you get back to your coffee," she said. "It was nice seeing you."

"You too." I pulled her in for another hug even though I wouldn't have normally done that. "Take care. You know you have a job at Steele and Steele whenever you're finished."

"You'll be the first person I call on graduation day." She gave me a quick hug before she walked out, smiling at me the entire time.

Not once did I look at Rose, trying to seem as infatuated as possible with a different woman. Then I grabbed my coffee and added a splash of cinnamon before I returned to the table, pretending like nothing just happened.

Rose's gaze was glued to the table so hard it was obvious she was forcing it.

Maybe she would try to get me back now that she knew I wouldn't always be available. "You ready to start?" I eyed my watch on my wrist. "I have plans later tonight." I didn't tell her what those plans were, letting her imagination run wild.

***

She was exceptionally quiet for the rest of the meeting. She didn't say anything unless she had to, and she didn't make eye contact with me either. Her heels crunched against the dirt ground as she walked further into the empty lot. Patches of grass and weeds were dispersed in random places.

She held the notebook in her hand and scribbled a few notes.

I walked around the lot and examined the two buildings adjacent on either side. The place was a good location, but the dimensions of the lot might make the design of the building a little difficult. I suspected Hawke paid a lot of money for the land—a fortune. I was glad he was reaching new levels of wealth. Not for his sake, but for Francesca's. If she wanted to quit her job and sell the bakery, she'd have that opportunity. She could stay home and raise their two kids. I suspected she would never do that, but it was nice to have the option.

Rose halted in the center of the lot and kept making notes. She wore dark jeans and a loose blouse. Her hair was done in curls and her makeup was done. She looked exceptional, like always. Just a week ago we slept together in the same bed, but now it seemed like we were a world apart.

I stayed quiet so I wouldn't disrupt her artistic thoughts. She was probably mapping out the entire place in her head, using that abnormally gifted brain of hers. She made a few more notes before she closed her notebook. "I think I have everything I need."

"Great." I walked with my hands in my pockets, appearing as casual as possible. "Just give one of us a call when you're ready to discuss your progress."

"I will."

We walked to the sidewalk. Fortunately, there wasn't any foot traffic in the area. I could feel the awkwardness rest on my shoulders. Naturally, I wanted to say something. I wanted to invite her to dinner or tell her I missed her. I wanted to convince her she was my soul mate, the one person I wanted to spend my life with. But I had to act like I didn't care. It was the only approach I hadn't tried. "Well, I guess I'll see you around." I nodded my head slightly in her direction then quickly turned around. It took all my strength to keep up the act, to pretend she didn't mean a damn thing to me.

"Kyle."

I turned around and kept up my poker face. "What's up?"

She held the notebook to her chest, a fight going on deep inside her. "Are you still mad at me?"

It was the dumbest thing I've ever heard her say. Was I having a conversation with a high school girl? "Why would I be mad at you?"

"The way we left things…"

"Rose, I'm over it. I'm not going to keep fighting for someone who doesn't want me. You've made your decision and I accept that. I worked my ass off to win that case for you, and I was the gentlest and most caring boyfriend the world has ever seen—but it wasn't enough for you. I'm not going to keep wasting my time on someone who doesn't deserve it." I kept my gaze cold, freezing her skin and everything beneath. Then I turned around and walked away without looking back. It was heartbreaking to act this way, to give her the cold shoulder in such a rude manner. But she didn't leave me any other choice. Either this would work or I would lose her altogether.

Sunday

CHAPTER SEVEN

Misery

Rose

When Kyle said he had plans later that night, did he have a date?

It was like a light had switched off in his head. He was one man, and then he completely changed the next instant. When we couldn't work it out, he turned cold—something I've never seen him do before. I understood his anger and frustration, but he didn't seem to care about my feelings at all.

It hurt.

Seeing him flirt with that blonde woman and possibly ask her on a date made me sick to my stomach. I still loved him and missed him, and to see him move on from me so quickly was nauseating. I wish we could work out our differences and move on, but that wasn't so simple for me.

Did he not understand that?

Florence called me one evening when I was sitting at home drinking a bottle of wine. "Hey, I heard about the trial in the paper."

"Good news, isn't it?"

"It is." She didn't sound too enthused about it. "Are you okay?"

"I'm glad he's in jail. And I'm glad he'll be there for the rest of his life. Of course I'm okay." I refilled my glass and took another drink.

"Then why do you sound so miserable?"

For entirely different reasons. "Kyle and I broke up."

"What?" she blurted into the phone. "I didn't know that. I'm sorry."

"It's okay…"

"What happened?"

I told her the truth, from the beginning to end.

"Whoa, hold on." Her attitude unleashed in full force. "He knew about Peter that entire time?"

"Most of the time."

"And he never said anything?"

"No." I was already halfway finished with the bottle of wine and I didn't intend to stop.

"And then he was the prosecutor for the trial?"

"Uh-huh."

"And he still didn't think about mentioning it to you?"

"Nope." I needed more wine.

"What kind of sick freak does that," she snapped. "What an asshole."

"He said he didn't want to scare me off by telling me the truth."

"Well, this is creepier."

"And then I slept with him..."

"You're serious?" she shrieked. "And even then he didn't tell you?"

"No." But Kyle was right when he pointed out I didn't tell him either.

"Fucking asshole." She seethed over the phone. "I'm going to murder him. Like, actually murder him."

"Don't bother." Our relationship was buried six feet under at this point.

"I really hate that guy," she said. "Will didn't say anything to me."

"I doubt he knows. Kyle wouldn't tell anyone." He wouldn't even tell me.

"I'm so sorry, girl. I could hear your sadness through the phone."

"I'll be okay. I've been through worse." There was one good thing about going through that trauma. I could take on everything else.

"There must be something I can do." Florence could be temperamental, but once someone she loved was in distress she was the most compassionate person on the planet. When I was at my worst, she stood beside me and helped me get back on my feet. Never once did she judge me or think less of me after that terrible night. She was stuck to me like glue.

"No. I'm okay."

"I met this really great guy last weekend. I'm sure he has a friend I could set you up with."

No more blind dates. "No, thank you." The last time I went on a blind date, Kyle walked inside and changed my world forever. I'll never forget that feeling at our initial meeting. The chills ran up and down my body, and even though I just met him I felt like I'd known him forever.

Every day after that was exactly the same. There was something pulling us together but I never understood what it was. Like magnet and steel, we were bound together. When I thought about our relationship I remembered all the inexplicable feelings that emerged between us. Something felt right the moment we met. He was the first man to make me believe in humanity again.

And I missed him.

***

I called Hawke and scheduled a meeting to go over the details of my design. He said he would be there in fifteen minutes. Part of me hoped Kyle would show up. But a different part of me, one deep within, hoped he would. We left things so awkward and I didn't want it to end that way.

Fifteen minutes later Hawke walked inside.

And Kyle was with him.

"I'm excited to see what you've created." Hawke rubbed his palms together greedily then sat down.

Kyle took the seat beside him, resting his ankle on the opposite knee and looking as stiff as his suit. He didn't look at me. He stared at the bookshelves next to my desk.

As hard as I tried to not let it bother me, it did. Did he go on a date the other night? Did he sleep with someone? "I think you'll like it." I turned the designs over to him, showing the sketches of the outside of the building.

Hawke stared at it without reacting. His face was a stone, cold wall. He rested his fingers on his bottom lip, his mind cut off from the world. Then he rubbed his chin gently, his wedding ring glinting under the florescent lights.

Now I started to feel nervous.

"Kyle, what do you think?" Hawke asked.

Kyle turned his focus to the sketch, taking it in silently. "I really like the exterior color. It'll stick out between the two other buildings and it looks sleek. The large ornate windows make it look inviting, but also prestigious. But the trimming around the windows and doors don't work well. I think we should make them something else, perhaps gray."

Hawke nodded. "I agree."

"And I think we should remove the sign over the door," Kyle said. "It's too big and desperate."

"Then how are they supposed to know what kind of business it is?" Hawke asked.

"You can put a sign, but make it small—elegant," Kyle said. "It says you're big enough that you don't need a sign."

Hawke nodded in agreement. "True. Let's make the changes."

It surprised me Hawke relied so much on Kyle's expertise. But then again, Kyle had been running a business on his own for a while.

"Can we see the rest?" Hawke asked.

"Sure." I turned the page and showed him the sketch of the lobby. I didn't show blueprints to customers because numbers and measurements wouldn't mean anything to them.

Hawke and Kyle both examined it.

Hawke's phone began to ring. "Sorry about that." He dug it out of his pocket.

"It's not a big deal," I said.

He eyed the screen then took the call. "Hey, Muffin. I'm in a meeting with the architect." His eyes still scanned the image. "Are you sure? I thought that was tomorrow?" He rubbed his temple and sighed. "Of course. My mistake. I'm on my way. Love you." He hung up and stuffed the phone into his pocket. "I'm sorry. I have to go. Kyle, you have this?"

"Don't worry about it," Kyle said automatically.

"Great." Hawke gave me an apologetic look. "I'm sorry. I forgot she and I had a meeting with our real estate agent."

"Is your daughter okay?" I blurted.

"She's fine," he said. "She's a fighter." He walked out and disappeared.

Now Hawke had left twice in a row. Was that a coincidence? Or was I being paranoid? I eyed Kyle suspiciously, wondering if I was being played without even realizing it. If this was a grand scheme it didn't seem that way. Kyle hadn't mentioned our relationship once. And it was clear he resented me and no longer wanted me back.

Kyle studied the page then turned it. "I like the inside. It's got a lot of open space."

"I think that's essential for a business like his. It's not about getting down to work. It's about giving his customers an experience of wealth." As an architect, I knew a lot about design. They went hand-in-hand in my line of business.

"And I like the floor plan for the offices. It's none of that cubicle stuff."

"Well, the cubicles will be on the second story. This is just an elaborate lobby because Hawke wanted it."

Kyle kept studying it with a trained eye. "The tile?"

"Hawke can choose that when they begin building. We don't need to pick that out right this second."

He rubbed his bottom lip as he continued to look at the drawing. He flipped to the last page, where the third story was mapped out. He took ten minutes to look at everything, to scrutinize it with stunning detail. "I think it looks good with the exception of the top floor."

"What's wrong with it?" I blurted, knowing I never messed up.

"I don't think the main office should be spaced out this way. Also, the bathroom is clear on the other side." He pointed his fingers along the hallway. "I think a break room should go here, alongside the bathroom. No one is going to be up there except Hawke and his workers."

"I think it's smart to have more than one bathroom…"

"That's not what I mean," he said with a laugh. "I just think this could be done better, frankly."

I took the blueprint back and examined it. "Okay. I'll make the changes." I realized just how personally I was taking this. None of my clients were happy with the first draft, but knowing Kyle didn't like it wounded me.

"Thank you." He spoke with the same tension, like he didn't like this conversation any more than I did. "I have something I want to discuss and it may be awkward..."

Was he going to ask about our relationship? His silence confused me, but now I realized it'd been lurking around the corner the entire time. "I'm listening."

"Since you already worked on the design to my beach house, did the design and the blueprint and everything, can we finish it? I could just start over with a new architect but that would be a serious waste of time and money. What do you say?"

That wasn't what I was expecting at all. "Uh, I don't see why not."

"Thank you. It would really make my life easier." He adjusted his cuff links without watching what he was doing. The movement was automatic.

That was all he wanted to say? Now that I was getting what I wanted, I realized I wanted it even less. "Did you want to work on that now? While you're here?"

"If you have the time." He dropped his sleeve then rested his hand on his knee. Most of the time he didn't even look at me.

Now it was hard to believe we were ever in love.

I grabbed the file then opened it on the desk. Everything was exactly as I left it. The drawings were only halfway completed, stunted the moment our relationship picked up. Now I had to finish it—but under different circumstances. "Where should we start?"

CHAPTER EIGHT

Deeper

Kyle

"I'm cutting you off." Will grabbed my Manhattan and pulled it away.

"Why?" Inexplicable rage clung to every word I said. "Dude, it's mine." I snatched it back and downed the rest of the glass. The migraine behind my eyes had dissipated because it was drowning in alcohol.

Will watched me warily, unsure how to stop me. "Everything okay, man?"

"Everything is fucking perfect." I tried to wave down the bartender to get another drink. "She acts like everything is just fine. It's like our break up doesn't affect her at all. How could she tell me she loved me then turn her back like that?"

Will bowed his head slightly. "I don't know, man. But I think we should get you home and talk about this there."

"I'm not going home," I snapped. "I'm going to live here—in this bar."

"Where will you shower?"

"I'll open a bottle and pour it over my head."

Will nodded. "I guess that could work."

I waved at the bartender again.

Will turned to her and shook his head.

The bartender continued to ignore me.

"Leave the nice lady alone," Will said. "You need a break."

"I'm thirsty."

"I don't see how that's possible," he said sarcastically.

"Alcohol makes you dehydrated. You didn't know that?" Random facts I thought I forgot about came back to me when I was loose like this.

"No. Thanks for the enlightenment."

I ran my fingers through my hair, feeling scorching hot everywhere. My skin burned and the collar around my throat was too tight. Sweat formed on my palms.

"Let's go home," Will said. "That tab is going to be too expensive for either one of us to pay."

I rested my chin on my palm. "I just don't get it…"

He gave me a sad look.

"I loved her. I loved her with everything I had. And she makes it look so easy, like it was so simple for her to walk away from me."

"I'm sure she's dying inside."

"It doesn't seem like it," I said bitterly. Was Francesca right? Were we really soul mates? If we were, wouldn't she feel just the way I did? Wouldn't she be suffering every single day? How could she work with me and not blink an eye over it?

"It'll be okay, man."

"No, it won't," I hissed.

"You're a catch. You can find someone else at the drop of a hat."

"But I don't want anyone else," I snapped. "Don't you get that?"

"Maybe you need to force yourself to want someone else…"

"You know what?" I pointed right at his face, making him flinch back slightly. "You're a lucky son of a bitch. You could have ended up with Rose and she would have broken your heart. I saved your ass. That woman is a goddamn man-eater."

Will grabbed my hand and gently pulled it away from his face. "Looks like I dodged a bullet, then."

"You did, my friend." I suck two fingers into my mouth and whistled loudly, making everyone in the bar look at me. "Sweetheart, can I get a drink or what?"

The bartender glared at me venomously before she continued her work.

Will ducked his head like he wanted to disappear.

"Stop your whining, you fucking pussy." A built guy from the next table turned in his chair and gave me the bird.

I could take him with one hand. "What'd you say, asshole?" I jumped to my feet.

Will cringed. "Goddammit."

"I said you're a pussy." He jumped to his feet and flexed his arms, ready to bash my skull in.

"I'm a pussy?" I asked incredulously. I grabbed the chair and held it up, prepared to use it as a weapon. "Say it again, bitch." I came around the table, ready to bash his skull in.

The guy grabbed his beer bottle and shattered it on the table, using the sharp shards as a weapon.

That didn't deter me at all.

"Whoa, calm down." Will grabbed the chair and pushed me back. "Kyle, knock it off."

"I'm going to kill this motherfucker."

Will pulled the chair from my grasp and dropped it on the ground. "With a criminal record, you could get debarred."

"I don't give a shit." I tried to grab the chair.

"Kyle, come on." Will grabbed me by the arm and dragged me out of the bar. "You're such a pain in the ass when you're drunk." He shoved me through the front doors and out to the sidewalk.

"What the hell? I can't just leave."

"You can. And you will." He kept his hold on my elbow and waved down a cab. "Let's get you home so you can't get into any more trouble."

"I can't just walk away from a fight." Beating the shit out of a stranger might make me feel better about losing Rose.

"Yes, you can." Will got a cab and threw me into the back. "Now shut up."

***

Will walked me inside my apartment then grabbed a bottle of water. "Drink this."

"Yuck."

"Stop being annoying and just do it." He shoved it into my chest.

I took a drink then leaned against the counter, feeling my body loosen in control. My legs didn't work the same anymore, and my brain didn't either. It took more effort to make logical connections.

"You should get into bed."

"It's not even eleven. Hell no, I'm not going to bed."

"Keep drinking."

I threw the bottle at him. "Go away, mother hen."

"I'm going to stay here for the night. You shouldn't be alone right now."

"Don't pity me." I walked into the living room and fell onto the couch.

Will followed me, taking the seat beside me. "I've never seen you this drunk before."

"That makes two of us..."

"Rose really fucked you up, huh?"

"I hate her." The ferocity left my throat, maniacal and frightening. "I hate everything about her. I hate her for coming into my life, and I hate her for still being in it."

Will stared at the blank TV.

My breathing increased and I lay back on the couch, feeling the room spin. I already knew I would throw up in just a few short hours. Tomorrow, I would have the greatest migraine known to man. And I'd feel like shit. "I don't hate her...I hate that I love her."

Will gave me a gentle pat on the shoulder.

"I'm meant to be with her. I just know. But she doesn't realize it yet...she doesn't know I'm her soul mate."

It was a testament to our relationship when Will didn't make fun of me.

"I don't think she'll ever realize it..." I leaned my head back and closed my eyes, trying to escape from my painful thoughts. Now all I wanted to do was fall asleep.

Will sat there, silent.

"You can go. I think my tantrum is over."

"You're sure? I can stay."

"No. I'm just a pain in the ass anyway." The room kept spinning and I tried to make it stop on my own. I hated myself in that moment, and I hated myself for not telling Rose the truth to begin with. How different my life could have been. I was so happy with her. And now I couldn't imagine ever being happy again.

CHAPTER NINE

Glide

Rose

This was exactly what I wanted.

I wanted Kyle to stop pursuing me. I wanted Kyle to give up on us and let me go. I wanted to move on with my life because I could never trust him again. But now that'd he given me what I wanted, I felt incomplete.

I spent my time alone in my apartment, watching basketball and hockey while wishing he were there. Anytime I went to work, I hoped he would stop by. When he seemed indifferent to me, I hoped it was all just an act.

Did I make a mistake?

Did I overreact and persecute him for an innocent act?

Was I wrong?

I couldn't picture myself being with anyone else. Kyle completed me in a way no one else ever had. Even before that terrible night, I never had a connection like that. In my heart I knew it meant something. For me to ever love someone after what happened was a miracle.

And Kyle was that miracle.

I stared at my phone before I grabbed it and typed a message. *Hey, do you think we can talk?* I stared at the message while my thumb hovered over the send button. It shook slightly with hesitation. Then I chickened out and deleted the message altogether.

I continued to sit in my living room as I tried to figure out what to do. I could just go to bed and try to forget about these feelings, but I wouldn't get any sleep anyway.

My heart was pounding in my chest, not in a good way. It was late in the evening but I knew Kyle would be awake. He didn't seem to go to bed until after midnight.

And I suspected he wasn't sleeping anyway, just the way I couldn't sleep.

Still filled with dread, I grabbed my stuff and walked out.

***

I waited in front of his door and stared at the wood. I raised my palm against it then quickly lowered it. Even if I did knock and he opened the door, what would I say? What would he say? Maybe this whole thing was a bad idea. But what if I went back to my apartment? What would that accomplish?

After debating for nearly ten minutes and wasting more time, I knocked. The sound thudded against my ears like an echo, and now I knew I couldn't take back what I just did. If he heard it, he would come.

Heavy footsteps erupted from the living room and they slowly approached the door. They approached too slowly, like it wasn't Kyle at all. Maybe someone else was in his apartment. I couldn't tell.

It took forever for the door to get unlocked. The lock was twisted and unlocked then locked again, and then he tried the door. It stayed in the panel because the lock was activated. Then he twisted back when he finally realized what the problem was.

What was going on here?

He opened the door and stumbled slightly, like he expected the door to be much lighter than it was. "Whoa..." He grabbed the door again and steadied himself. It took him a second to focus his attention on me. He stared at me without any realization. It was as if he was staring at a blank wall. Heartbeats passed, and slowly the familiarity stretched across his face. "Real...or not real?"

"Real."

He continued to hold onto the door for balance.

Something was off. He wasn't himself in the least. "Kyle, are you okay?"

"Fine." He rubbed his temple with a sigh. His eyes were bloodshot and he had an unnatural stance. He swayed like he was in a dream.

"Are you drunk...?"

"No...yes...no." He rubbed his eye to remove the sleep particles. Then his voice suddenly turned hostile. "What do you want?"

"Uh..." He'd never spoken to me like that, even when he was at his worst moment. "I just—"

"Just what?" he asked. "Came back here because you're lonely? Came back because you want something? Bored? You'll be here for five minutes, get the assurance you need, and then you'll be on your way again. Rose, I may be a sappy and sensitive guy, but I don't let any woman just walk all over me and take me for a ride. So whatever it is you want, I'm not giving it to you."

I let the insults wash over me, but a few of them seeped deep into my skin.

"Now leave me alone, Rose. You've terrorized me enough." He shut the door in my face and locked it.

I heard the audible click as the lock turned. Then his footsteps drifted away into the background. I heard an audible fall as his body hit the couch. Even though he wasn't going to open the door again, I stood there. Now I understood just how much I hurt him—how much this break up hurt both of us.

***

I didn't speak to Kyle for the next few days. He didn't call me, not that I expected him to. But he was on my mind constantly. I was certain he was drunk that night, but his state didn't really make a difference. He meant every word he said.

I was sitting in my office when Kyle walked inside, looking just as pissed off as he did the other night. He carried a folder under his arm and immediately plopped down into the chair without giving a single greeting. "Busy?"

Were we down to one-word sentences now? "No."

"Hawke wanted me to drop this off." He tossed the folder across the desk. "They're the changes he wants. That man is meticulous so I expect he'll be making several more changes before this project is complete."

I opened the folder and flipped through the pages. "That's fine. I want my clients to get exactly what they want."

"Good." Instead of marching out he stayed put. "Do you have any progress on my place?"

"Uh, yeah." I opened my drawer and pulled out a file. "I've made a few more additions."

He flipped through the pages and studied each detail. "Why are there only four bedrooms?"

"I thought you said you only needed four."

"I never said that. I said I need a house for a family of four."

"Then what's the purpose of the last bedroom?"

"An office," he said. "My wife will need one."

"And you won't?"

"No. I never work from home but she does."

She does? Did he already know who his wife was? "Uh...what?"

"I mean, I assume she'll work from home most of the time." He turned the page. "So, I want white shelves constructed into the walls, and I want a large window that looks over the beach. It needs to be on the opposite side of where the kids' bedrooms are. I don't want them to disturb her."

"Okay..."

"And for the master bedroom, I want a walk-in closet."

"I didn't realize you needed that."

"But she will. It's every woman's dream, right?"

"I suppose."

"I want this house to have everything. Since we're building it from the ground up, we may as well include everything. It's not like we can go back and change it."

"Actually, you can."

"I prefer to have everything done. Which brings me to my next point. I want a pool. Every beach house should have a pool, right? That way my kids can have all their friends over in the summer."

He'd been putting a lot of thought into this. Did he have a date recently? And did that date go well? Is that why he shut the door in my face the other night? His demeanor was exactly the same as it used to be. It was like that night never happened.

"Is that cool?" he asked.

"Whatever you want, I can make it happen."

"Good attitude." He turned the page again. "I want an outside fireplace and I also want a pizza oven in the kitchen."

"You like pizza?"

"Yeah. But I suspect she will too."

I made the notes.

He turned the page again. "That's all I can think of for now. Not sure if I want a hot tub or not."

"It gets pretty cool in the evenings."

"True. Yeah, throw that in there too."

"These changes will affect the cost." I'm sure he knew that but I had to say it anyway.

"No problem."

"Okay." I made a list of all the changes he wanted.

"I'll leave this for you." He shut the folder and pushed it toward me. "Give me a call whenever you're finished."

Were we not going to mention what happened the other night? Was it that insignificant to him? "Kyle?"

"Hmm?" When he stood up he buttoned the front of his jacket before he straightened his tie. He hardly looked at me anymore, like I was someone not worth paying attention to.

"About the other night...I'm sorry I stopped by."

"Stopped by where?" he asked in a bored voice.

Did he not remember? He was drunk that night—the drunkest I've ever seen him. Did he black out the second I left? "Your apartment..."

"You stopped by?" he asked. "Why?"

So, he really didn't remember. "I just...wanted to drop off some paperwork."

"Oh. Well, just mail them to me next time." He headed to the door.

It was like we never loved each other. It was like we never had that connection. It was like...we never meant anything.

"See ya." He said the words without looking back, and then he walked out.

I suddenly felt the urge to cry, to weep as hard and loud as I could. Going our separate ways was the best for both of us, but then why did I feel so terrible deep inside?

Why did I feel like I'd never be happy again as long as I lived?

***

It took me a few days to make the changes he requested, and by the time I did, I was feeling worse. Now doubt plagued my mind every second of the day. I questioned my own reasoning and logic.

I questioned my own heart.

When I called him, I felt the nerves get to me as they always did. I listened to the phone ring endlessly, wondering if he would pick up. He always did, so why would it be any different now?

"Steele."

That was his last name but I never heard him introduce himself that way before. "Kyle?"

"What's up?" I heard voices in the background.

"I have the changes for the beach house."

"Oh okay," he said in a bored voice. "Can you drop them off at my office? I'm swamped today."

"Yeah, I—"

Click.

Sunday

I listened to the line go dead. The phone was still held to my ear and the sound echoed loudly. I slowly put it down and felt the blood drain from my veins. My greatest fear was true. I really did mean nothing to him.

It took nearly half an hour for me to gather my bearings and find the courage to go over there. The cold way he brushed me off was forever ingrained in my mind. We went from needing each other desperately to tossing each other aside like garbage.

I walked into his office and realized I hadn't been there since my own trial. The firm was called Steele and Steele but I never made the connection with Kyle's last name. Actually, I didn't know what it was until just a few moments ago. The memories came flooding back. I worked with Mark in his office, preparing to take the stand as a witness and give my testimony. Actually, I spent a lot of time there. I wondered if I'd met Kyle's father without realizing it.

"Can I help you?" The secretary looked up at me, a beautiful blonde woman.

"Hi...I'm here to see Kyle."

"Mr. Steele?" she corrected. "Do you have an appointment?"

"No. But he asked me to stop by and bring him something. Did he mention I was coming?"

"No." She stared at me like I was gum on the bottom of her shoe.

"Oh..." I gripped the folder in my hands, feeling smaller and smaller by the second.

His office door opened and he stepped out. "Thanks for coming by. I'll see you later."

A brunette woman that made me look like a troll stepped out with him. "We should get dinner."

Kyle glanced at me when he noticed I was there. "Yeah. Sounds like a good idea." He gave her a quick kiss on the cheek before he smiled.

She waved then walked off, wearing heels that were so tall she would break her ankle if she took one wrong step.

Kyle's smile disappeared when he looked at me. "Come in." Instead of waiting for me he walked inside and left the door open.

I was still processing what I witnessed. He kissed her on the cheek, showing her affection that could be friendly or something more. I wanted to know which it was but realized I had no right to ask.

"So, you're done?" He sat behind his desk and extended his hand to the folder.

With a shaky hand, I gave it to him.

He opened it and quickly browsed through it like he wanted to get this over with as quickly as possible. "It looks good but not exactly what I imagined." He grabbed a pencil then marked up the paper. "The fireplace should be here...I want the pool to face this way...and I want the shelves in the walk-in closet to be a little bigger. You know, so she can put her boots inside."

Was the woman he wanted to be with that woman who just left? Did he picture her as his future wife? Was I forgotten that easily? I never wore heels like that, and I certainly didn't have that kind of confidence. "Okay..." I stood there awkwardly, feeling my heart race painfully.

He made a few more notes before he shut the folder. "Let me know when you're done." He slid the folder across the surface then grabbed his phone.

For a moment I couldn't move. This kind of pain has never wrecked my body before. I felt sick—really sick. I questioned everything, wondering what we really had. Did I make up the whole thing?

Kyle finally looked up. "Rose? You all right?"

"Yeah..." I snapped out of it and grabbed the folder. "I'm fine." I grabbed the corner and the papers fell across the ground, making a mess.

Kyle didn't get up.

I ducked down and gathered everything, grateful I could hide my face for a moment. Now all the papers were out of order but at least they were all inside. I was a clumsy fool letting my emotions get the best of me.

I held the folder against my chest so I wouldn't drop them again. "Well, I'll see you around..." I kept my head bowed and turned to the door.

"Are you sure you're okay?" he asked. "Because you look paler than a ghost."

"I'm fine. Just remembered I have a meeting in my office right now."

"Alright. See you later." He turned to his computer and didn't even notice my absence.

CHAPTER TEN

The Plan

Kyle

I walked into the bakery and met Francesca in the cake kitchen. "What the hell are you making?" It was a cake covered with nude figures. The women had noticeable breasts, and the men had their junk dangling between their legs.

"It's a cake." She set the last figurine on the tier.

"I figured that out. But what's with the naked people?"

"This couple met on a nude beach in Barcelona."

I raised an eyebrow. "And they want people to know that...?"

She shrugged. "Whatever. It's their day."

I couldn't imagine my mom eating a piece of my wedding cake if it looked like that.

Francesca removed her apron and washed her hands. "How's the plan going?"

"I have no goddamn idea." This was blowing up in my face. All I wanted was to get her back, but all I'd succeeded in doing was pushing her further away. "She came by my office yesterday and saw me kiss one of my pretty clients on the cheek. She was really flustered after that, dropping everything and being quiet."

"Isn't that a good thing?"

I shrugged then fell into the chair at the table. "I don't know. It seemed like it bothered her, but not bothered her enough to want me back. I don't get it...what do I have to do?" I was running out of options. "She said something about coming to my apartment the other night but I have no idea what she's talking about."

"When did this happen?"

"Last week, I think."

"Were you not home?"

"She said I was. But I don't remember the conversation."

She grabbed a few muffins then set them on the table before she sat down. "How can you not remember it? Unless you were drunk."

"Well...last week I went out with Will. I got pretty wasted."

"Oh no."

"Maybe that's what she's referring to." I had no idea what I might have said. I was temperamental and angry at the time, but I must not have said anything too bad because she was still designing the house. "I don't know what to do, Frankie. I think I give up."

"You can't give up, Kyle."

"Maybe I love her. Maybe I'm supposed to be with her. But those things don't mean anything if she doesn't feel the same way."

"Give it time."

"I've given it plenty of time," I said with a sigh. "I've been cold to her and I've acted like I'm seeing other women. I've done everything necessary to make it seem like she doesn't mean anything to me. What else can I do?"

Francesca remained silent because she was stumped.

"There's nothing else." I didn't mind chasing the girl. It was the most thrilling part. But this was just sad. "I give up."

Francesca didn't object.

"I know relationships aren't perfect, but this is the opposite extreme. I can't make her be with me, and I'm not going to keep wasting time trying to convince her to be with me. So...I'm done." The finality of the words hit me hard in the chest. I was closing one chapter of my life and moving onto the next. "Done."

Francesca gave me a sad look. "Kyle..."

"I just want a nice girl who loves me. That's it. Who knew that would be so hard to find...?"

"It's not. You'll find the right person eventually. I promise."

"You can't make a promise like that..."

She placed her hand over mine. "Actually, I can."

CHAPTER ELEVEN

Stopping By

Rose

I stayed home for the next few days, eating everything in my kitchen until there wasn't anything edible left. Only the expired products remained behind, and I wasn't that desperate—yet.

I spent most of my time on the couch because I hated my bed. Kyle used to sleep in there with me. Without him beside me there was no point in being in there. It was just a reminder that he was gone.

Even if I wanted him back it was too late. He'd moved on with his life. I couldn't blame him for it. Our relationship was complicated, to say the least, but he was a good guy throughout the duration. Whoever ended up with him would be a very lucky woman.

And that woman wouldn't be me.

The problems of our past still bothered me, but I couldn't deny that I lost a great man. He was the first person that made me believe in happiness again. Now that he was gone, that joy disappeared.

Pieces of stale popcorn were sprinkled all over the couch, and some were stuck underneath the cushions. The scent of butter was in the air, and since I hadn't cleaned in so long the place was starting to smell like a cafeteria.

Someone knocked on my door.

I immediately hoped it was Kyle. No one else ever stopped by my place. If anyone wanted to see me, they texted. I was in sweats and a t-shirt, not my finest attire. Now I hoped it wouldn't be Kyle.

When I looked through the peephole, I saw a brunette woman standing there. She had long hair pulled into a braid over one shoulder. Her skin was fair, as vibrant as a porcelain doll. I didn't recognize her at all. But I recognized the man she was with. It was Hawke.

I opened the door and crossed my arms over my chest like that would make my clothing less hideous. "Hi...what's going on?" How did Hawke know where I lived? I couldn't recall mentioning it.

"Hey," Hawke said. "This isn't a bad time, right?"

"Depends. What's up?"

The woman had her eyes trained on me. "May we come in?"

"I guess." I stepped aside and allowed them to walk in.

"This is my wife, Francesca," Hawke said.

"Oh." I should have assumed. "It's nice to meet you." I quickly shook her hand, feeling self-conscious for having my hair in a messy bun.

"You too," she said politely.

Hawke had his arm around her waist. His large hand made her look smaller in comparison. "How are you?"

"Good," I lied. "Just taking the day off..." Why didn't he go to my office? Why did he come here? "How's your little one?"

"She's perfect." Francesca's voice immediately changed from serious to happy. "She's staying with her aunt right now."

"Cool," I said. "So, how can I help you?"

Hawke eyed Francesca, yielding the floor to her.

"I came here to talk about Kyle." She stepped away from Hawke's embrace and came closer to me.

"Kyle?" His name hurt on the way out.

"Yeah. Can we sit down?"

How did she know him? Through Hawke? "Sure..."

We sat down in the living room and Hawke stayed in the kitchen. He sat down and pulled out his phone, busying himself with correspondence. Why was he staying there while Francesca talked alone? I didn't even know her.

"I've known Kyle for a long time," she began. "And I can honestly say he's one of the most caring, compassionate, and gentle men I've ever known in my life. If he's done something to hurt you, I can promise you it wasn't on purpose."

I didn't expect her to say any of that. "I don't understand where this is coming from..."

"Kyle has been going through a hard time, and he's come to us for support. Having you work on my husband's new office was just a rouse to get you to spend time with him. But when Kyle realized this was only pushing you further apart, he lost hope. Now he doesn't have any belief in the two of you."

Everything was set up? Hawke didn't need an office at all?

Francesca read my thoughts through my eyes. "Hawke needs the office regardless. Kyle just asked him to hire you and keep him as a consultant. So, he misled you but not entirely."

I didn't know what to make of this. It was a trick and I walked right into it.

"The truth is, Kyle is absolutely miserable without you. And I know you're miserable without him."

I bowed my head in acknowledgment.

"I understand why you're hurt after everything that happened. Kyle lied to you and withheld important information. But it was never for malicious intent. It was a delicate situation and he didn't know how to handle it. There's no possible way you could think of him as a liar and a manipulator. Just look at what he does for a living. He represents victims who can't represent themselves."

I knew he was a great person. That was never the problem.

"Give him another chance before it's too late."

"I don't understand why you're the one to tell me all of this. I'm sorry, but I don't know you."

"Well..." She glanced at her husband before she turned back to me. "Kyle and I were together for about a year."

She dated him? I couldn't keep the shock off my face.

"And he was the most amazing man. He treated me like a queen every single day. If I hadn't already found my one true love, I would have married Kyle. So, of all people, I understand how great he is. And frankly, if you don't get this together soon you're going to lose your chance forever. Guys like Kyle aren't as common as you think. They're rare—unheard of. If you love this man and want to be with him, don't waste any more time. Tell him how you feel."

A part of me was jealous that she'd been with the man I loved, but then I realized that jealousy was misplaced when I saw her with Hawke. Everything she said was the truth. Kyle was the greatest man I'd ever find, and it was stupid to let him slip through my fingers. "He doesn't feel the same way anymore...he's indifferent to me."

"That's not true."

"It is. You haven't seen him with me. I came to his apartment a few weeks ago to talk about our relationship, and he told me to get out of his life before he shut the door in my face."

Recognition came onto her face. "He was drunk and not himself at the time. I can promise you, if you ask for another chance, he'll give it to you. But that offer won't last forever so you need to get on it."

I looked down at my hands in my lap.

Francesca continued to stare at me. "I know you've been through a lot but pushing away the man who's been nothing but loyal to you isn't the answer. It's normal to be scared, but it's not normal to be a coward. Make this work and don't lose him."

My heart was quickening and my palms were growing sweaty.

"If you don't want him, someone else will snatch him. If you don't want that to happen, then you need to speak to him. Everything is on the line here."

I couldn't forget my last interaction with him. He was so cold—chilling. "Are you sure?"

"Sure of what?"

"Sure that he even wants that..." He kissed some woman on the cheek, flirted with another one in that coffee shop, and then acted as if I didn't matter to him.

"Rose, I'm absolutely sure. Talk to him."

I was still on the fence.

"I know you don't know me, but trust me on this. Go to him and tell him how you feel. The conversation might be strenuous at first, but you guys will make it through. All he wants is for the two of you to get back together."

"I don't understand why he wants me so much..." I knew why I wanted him—because he was perfect. But I was damaged goods.

"You do, Rose." She gave me a knowing look. "You do."

***

After I showered and removed the bits of popcorn from my hair, I showed up on his doorstep. It wasn't nine just yet, but in just a few minutes it would be. I stared at his door as I had a hundred times already. Last time I was here the conversation didn't go over well.

Hopefully, that wouldn't happen again.

I knocked on the door then swallowed the lump in my throat.

Nothing but silence ensued inside. I waited for something to happen, for the sound of moving footsteps, but they never came. Even though it was clear he wasn't home I stayed on the doorstep. I could call him but I didn't want to have this conversation on the phone. I could wait until he came home but how long would I be standing outside?

"I was impressed when you caught the piece of shrimp in your mouth." A woman's voice drifted from the end of the hallway.

"Well, I practice." Kyle chuckled at his own comment.

"I had a great time tonight." When they rounded the corner they were holding hands. It was a pretty blonde girl with heels I could never pull off. She was close to his side, invading every inch of his personal space.

I felt sick to my stomach.

I wanted to run and hide but there was nowhere for me to go. On my side there was a dead-end. The only way out was to pass by them, but there was no way I could do that without being seen.

"I had a great time too." Kyle guided her to his door then stopped when he spotted me standing outside. He couldn't hide the surprise stretching across his face. His eyes were full of confusion, and he looked awkward and out of place.

I remained rooted to the spot, wishing I would just die in that moment.

His date eyed us back and forth, unsure what was going on.

"Rose...what are you doing here?" Kyle dropped her hand and took a step away from her.

"I..." I eyed the woman with him, so painfully beautiful it made me look plain in comparison, and then I felt the fear grip me by the throat. I couldn't say what I came here to say. Now it was too difficult—impossible. I missed my chance. "I came here to tell you I need more time with the design." It was the lamest excuse ever but it was all I could think of at the moment.

"Okay..." He glanced at his date then turned back to me.

"But I'll get it done as soon as I can...have a good night." I pushed past the girl and headed down the hallway, trying to get away from both of them as quickly as possible. I rounded the corner then leaned against the wall, feeling the tears burn deep in my eyes. Seeing him with someone else, officially moved on, was the most painful thing I've ever seen.

"So...who was that?" the woman asked.

Kyle's voice was still shaken. "You remember that woman I told you about?"

"Rose? The woman you're still in love with?"

"Yeah."

"Oh...does she normally stop by like that?"

"No. I'm not sure what that was about."

After a long pause she said, "Well...should we go inside?"'

"Yeah, of course." Kyle fished his keys out of his pocket and got the door unlocked.

I remained against the wall, processing everything I just heard. Kyle was still in love with me, but he was seeing other people. He was trying to get over me, to forget about me forever. There was still hope we could find our way back to each other—but only if I acted now. If he slept with her it would break my heart so irrevocably it could never be put back together. I couldn't stand the sight of him just holding her hand, let alone anything else.

I had to do something—even though I was terrified to do it.

I walked back to his apartment, feeling the thud of every footstep. My heart was lodged deep in my throat and my lungs weren't working correctly. I felt a stomachache come on from all the stress.

I stopped in front of his door and tried to breathe.

I had to do this.

I could do this.

It was now or never.

I knocked and took a step back.

The woman's voice came from inside. "Do you want me to get that?"

"I got it." Kyle's footsteps approached the door.

Oh my god. Oh my god. Oh my god.

He opened it, and judging the look on his face he didn't expect to see me. "Rose?"

My hands were locked together in front of my waist so they would stop shaking. My chest ached painfully from my rapid breathing. The tears were still present, buried deep beneath. "I'm sorry to bother you..."

Kyle stared at me, confused as ever.

I didn't know where to start or what to say, so I just said whatever came to mind. "I want to get back together. I don't want you to be with anyone else. I'm sorry I broke up with you in the first place. It was stupid and unfair. I was just scared and not thinking clearly. I'm sorry I took so long to tell you but I'm telling you now. If there's any hope for us...give me a chance."

That same look didn't leave his face. Now he wasn't just confused, but surprised.

Was Francesca wrong when she said he would take me back? Did she make an assumption she shouldn't have made? Even if she told me otherwise, I'd probably still be standing here. If there were any hope for us I'd have to try. I didn't want him to spend the night with this woman. The thought would give me eternal nightmares.

Kyle still didn't speak, his hand still resting on the door.

"Please tell me I'm not too late." Was he over me? Had he moved on? Was I the last person he thought about?

"No, you're never too late." He stepped into the hallway and closed the door behind him. Then he cupped my face, his fingers lightly digging into my hair just the way they used to. His face was close to mine and he looked deep into my eyes. His thumb moved across my cheek until it rested in the corner of my mouth. "You forgive me?"

"There's nothing to forgive...I wish I realized that sooner."

"You're sure about this? Rose, it hurt enough when you walked away the first time. My heart couldn't bare it if you walked away again." It was the first time he showed any weakness to me. For the past month he'd been brutally aggressive and indifferent. But now the Kyle I knew shined through.

"I'm here to stay."

Finally, a smile broke his lips. He pulled me into his chest and hugged me tightly. His heavy arms wrapped around my torso and crushed me against him. His chin rested on the top of my head, and he released a deep sigh of contentment.

"I'm so sorry…"

"Shh." He rubbed the area between my shoulder blades then the back of my neck.

I melted in his arms, missing the way this comfort used to feel. I once had the liberty of doing this whenever I wanted, and I threw it away because I couldn't think straight. His cologne washed over me, reminding me of passionate nights we used to share. His hard chest felt exactly the way it used to when I lay on top of him in bed. All the memories came flooding back, heightened by his return.

The front door opened and his date emerged. "Kyle—" She fell silent when she realized what we were doing.

I immediately pulled away at getting caught but Kyle didn't.

She gave him the stink eye before she shut the door.

"I'm sorry..." I'd forgotten about her.

"Don't worry about it." His eyes were glued to me the entire time and he reluctantly let me go.

"I should go..."

He clearly didn't want that to happen. "I'll come over after I talk to her."

"Okay." I looked at the ground because a terrible thought came into my mind. I wondered if he'd slept with her. It clearly wasn't their first date, and that woman wasn't immune to Kyle's perfection. But I didn't ask because I had no right to know.

Like always, Kyle read my mind. "I kissed her—that's all."

I looked up, feeling the relief swim through my body.

He gave me a slight smile before he walked back inside.

My body started to come back to life. I was getting a second chance of being happy. If Kyle didn't love me so much I would have lost everything. But thankfully, he loved me more than I could ever comprehend.

***

Kyle didn't come by for hours. It was nearly midnight and he still hadn't stopped by. He was probably having a difficult conversation with his date. He definitely didn't come off good in the situation.

He finally knocked on the door. "Sweetheart, it's me."

"Come in." I jumped off the couch but lost my balance for a moment, my legs moving quicker than my body was ready for.

He walked inside and shut the door behind him. "Sorry about that..."

"It's okay." I stood in front of him, unsure what to do with my hands. They met together in front of my waist then moved behind my back. Then I crossed my arms over my chest but that wasn't comfortable either. He made me nervous as hell. "I hope everything is okay."

"Lea wasn't happy." He eyed me with the old fondness that used to shine in his eyes.

"I'm sorry. I feel so bad..." Part of me judged me for going after a guy who was on a date with another woman.

But the bigger part of me didn't care because I wanted him so badly. In my eyes, he was still mine.

"Don't."

"I should have realized this sooner...could have avoided all of this."

"I'd rather you wait until you're sure than rush it." He put his hands in his pockets, keeping a few feet between us. "And she knew I was in love with you. When we started seeing each other, I was honest about that. But, I also told her you and I were never getting back together...I think that's why she was a little blind-sided."

"Oh..." I kept my arms tight around my chest.

He kept the distance between us as he stared at me.

I stared back, suddenly terrified of what was about to happen.

"So...are you going to kiss me or what?" That handsome smile stretched his lips, his boyish charm coming to the surface.

I chuckled because I realized how stupid I must have looked. "Of course." I dropped my arms and closed the gap between us.

He stared at me with longing, memorizing every detail of my face.

My hands moved to his stomach and I slowly moved them up, feeling his hard abs and then the slab of concrete known as his chest. I felt his distant beating heart, noting how calm it was. I reached his shoulders and felt the definition of muscle, remembering the way I would grab onto them when we made love. My fingers moved up his neck then cupped his face, feeling the resistance of his facial hair. His blue eyes were sparkling with excitement, and he looked absolutely beautiful.

He didn't lean in for the kiss, letting me do all the work.

"I missed you."

"I missed you too, sweetheart." His hands snaked around my waist.

"You were so cold to me...I thought you hated me."

"Hate you?" he whispered. "Never. I was just trying to make you think I did."

"Well, you succeeded."

"I was really angry, but I never hated you."

I felt the skin just below his lip, feeling the softness. "I'm sorry I took off. I'm sorry I put so much pressure on you. I just got upset and I didn't know what to do."

"I understand, Rose. It was a difficult situation. No one can comprehend the circumstance unless they've been in it themselves."

He was always so patient with me, so understanding. "I'm sorry I hurt you."

"It's okay. Now that we're together it feels like a bad dream."

My lips ached for his but I didn't move in. Feeling his embrace was enough to give me the high I craved. Whenever we were together like this I felt that heat in my blood. It did funny things to my body.

He glanced at my lips, waiting for the embrace.

I pressed my mouth to his and felt the explosion like always. A stick of dynamite had been lit inside me, and it exploded into a million pieces of fiery ash. The explosion rippled everywhere throughout my body. I felt high, higher than I'd ever been.

His lips felt exactly the way they used to, warm and soft. His facial hair rubbed against me gently, enticing me. Somehow, I found it innately sexy. My breathing immediately quickened because I wasn't getting enough oxygen to fuel the spike of adrenaline. My fingers dug into his shoulders and I felt my knees grow weak. He made me aroused in just a nanosecond. I wasn't sure how that was possible.

He grabbed my hips and gently steered me toward my bedroom, still kissing me as he went. He felt my lips lovingly, and every kiss was purposeful and delicious. My bottom lip trembled when he sucked it, and my panties suddenly became damp.

He guided me on the bed then slowly stripped my clothes away. He started with my shoes then moved to my jeans.

I wanted him—badly. But I wasn't ready to jump back into bed, not yet anyway. I didn't stop him because I suspected he knew that. So I let him be, stripping my clothes away until I was completely naked on the bed.

He pulled his shirt off and kept kissing me, and then my hands worked his jeans until they were loose. I got them off and took the boxers with them. When they reached his ankles he kicked them away.

We got under my covers then wrapped our bodies around one another. My legs were tight around his waist and I felt his hard-on rub against me every time he moved. He kissed me aggressively on the mouth, giving me some of his tongue. Then he would stop altogether and rub his nose against mine, looking into my eyes like he wanted to stop just to look at me. Then he would kiss me slowly until the pace picked up again.

My hands memorized every feature of his body, feeling the definition of muscle along his back and shoulders. My thighs squeezed his hips, remembering the way he used to thrust into me as I held on.

His lips moved to my neck and he kissed me everywhere while his other hand dug into my hair. Despite his aggression he didn't make a move for something more. Despite how hard he was he didn't try to make love to me. He kept kissing me, understanding that was all I was ready for at the moment. To me, it was just as good as sex—perhaps even better.

My fingers felt his strands of hair and I felt the words escape my lips. "I love you." I spoke them directly into his mouth, feeling them get drowned out in our kiss. "I love you too."

CHAPTER TWELVE

Happiness

Kyle

Rose was mine again.

She showed up on my doorstep when I least expected it, and she asked me to take her back. After my last interaction with her, I didn't think that would happen. I thought we were done—for good.

And then I was wrong.

I woke up that morning with her cradled in my arms. She was naked just the way I was, and I loved feeling our bare skin rub together like this. Even without sex I was happy. I was just happy being there with her.

Lea was pissed when I told her we were done. Even though we hadn't been seeing each other long, she was into me. She was so into me that she didn't care if I was still hung up on my ex. I felt terrible ending our relationship the way I did, especially with Rose standing right outside.

But I had to do the right thing.

Rose was the woman I loved. Even though she left me high and dry, I couldn't get over her. And I didn't have the strength to say no out of principle. My heart would be on its guard unlike last time but I was still in the relationship nonetheless.

Rose stirred a few moments later, her hair all over the place. Her fingers felt the skin of my ribs before her eyes opened. It took her a few seconds for her eyes to focus. But when they did, a small smile spread across her face. "Morning."

"Morning." I snuggled into her side and kissed her shoulder. "Sleep well?"

"I haven't slept like that in forever." She tightened my arm around her waist and rested her hand over mine.

"Then I should sleep here every night."

"You won't hear any objections from me." She placed a kiss over the skin of my heart.

I felt my hair stand on end. "I like it when you kiss me like that."

"Then I'll do it more often."

I had to go to the office that day and take care of a few things, but I was seriously tempted to blow it off. There was nothing I'd rather do than stay here all day—with her.

"I have to work...but I don't want to go."

"Me too," I said. "We can both play hooky."

"I would but I have a meeting. Unless I'm sick, I don't see how I can reschedule it."

"Well, as soon as we're both finished we can come straight back here."

"That's a pretty good idea." She rubbed my chest.

I loved this moment. I wanted it to stay just like this forever—and ever. "What made you change your mind?" I was so happy she was there I didn't really think about it.

She continued to rub my chest as she stared at it, taking her time before she answered. "It's a long story..."

"Well, I've got time." I wanted to hear her answer. It didn't seem like I stood a chance of getting her back just last week.

"A few weeks ago I missed you so much it was killing me. So I went to your apartment but you...weren't yourself. You told me you were sick of my shit and told me to leave you alone. After that, I was too scared to say anything. I thought I screwed up and couldn't get you back."

When did this happen? I had no recollection of it. "What? I don't remember this."

"I think you were drunk. But even when we're drunk we tell the truth. So...I tried to leave you alone."

I remembered I went drinking with Will and woke up the next morning on the couch with all my clothes still on. I didn't have a memory from that night, just bits and pieces. That must have been the night she was referring to. "I'm sorry...I was out of my mind that night. I don't even remember this conversation. That's how wasted I was."

She nodded in agreement.

"Then what happened?"

"I accepted the fact I lost you and tried to move on. Then Hawke and Francesca—"

"Whoa, what?" How did she know who Francesca was? I was so surprised by her words that I interrupted her from finishing. Something happened right under my nose and I didn't even realize it.

"Hawke and Francesca came to my apartment yesterday. They told me we should be together, and if I didn't do something soon I would lose you forever. And Francesca said you would take me back."

I couldn't believe Francesca did that. She didn't even tell me. "What else did she say?"

"That you two used to be together." She avoided eye contact with me when she mentioned that part. "And if Hawke wasn't her soul mate, she would have married you. She said you were one of the greatest guys she's ever met, and I'd be lucky to have you."

She really did that? I was speechless.

"She didn't convince me to be with you. I knew where I wanted to be. But she gave me the courage to say something. If she hadn't, I would have run away the second I saw you with Lea. I would have thrown in the towel and given up."

I still couldn't believe she did that for me. Francesca hurt me a lot in the past. She left me for Hawke. And then she left me again—a second time. I was heartbroken for a while, unable to move on because I was so devastated. But her actions made up for all of that. She wanted me to be happy, to have what she had with Hawke. Even though we'd been broken up for so long she still loved me—as a friend. "I'm glad she said something to you."

"Me too." She ran her fingers through my hair and looked into my eyes. "I admit it's a little awkward knowing you two used to love each other but...it doesn't seem relevant anymore."

"It's not." Now that I'd found the right person to share my life with, everything else faded away.

"So...does that mean you no longer need me to work on Hawke's office?"

"No, I do. We both do."

"And your beach house?"

I had specific plans for that in mind. "I still need you for that too."

A slow smile crept her lips. "You have me. You don't need to make up stuff to keep me around."

"I know. But I really think you're the best woman for the job."

***

I walked in the back kitchen of the bakery and saw Francesca standing at the table where mixing bowls sat. A bag of flour was right beside them. "I need to talk to you."

She nearly jumped in the air when she realized she wasn't alone. "Shit, you scared me." She clutched her chest and got powder everywhere.

"Sorry, not sorry." I stood in front of her and crossed my arms over my chest. "Rose told me what you said to her."

She didn't look guilty at all. She looked me in the eye, fearless like always. "I hope some good came from it."

"She asked me to take her back—which I did."

"Then why do you seem so stern today?"

"Because I can't believe you did that for me." My fondness for Francesca would never die. I respected her a person as well as a former lover.

"Kyle, you know I would do anything for you. While our relationship didn't work out, I cared about you a lot. I want nothing but the best for you. And I want you to have what I have with Hawke."

"I know. But I still can't believe you intervened like that."

"Sometimes relationships need help. I know Hawke and I needed a lot of it."

I chuckled. "You could say that again."

"So you guys are back together?"

"Yeah." I smiled just thinking about it.

"I'm glad. Did you tell her how you feel?"

I knew she was referring to my belief we were soul mates. "No. I want her to figure it out on her own. And I'm afraid it might scare her off it I tell her. I want to be with her and hope we can make this work. But honestly, my guard is up."

"Why?"

"I'm afraid she'll run out on me again." She would have to regain my trust to cure my paranoia. When she left I was devastated. "To avoid going through that again, I think I'll always be prepared for the worst."

"I'm sure she won't make the same mistake twice."

"Hopefully." I couldn't bare it if she did.

She removed her apron and tossed it on the counter. "So, why are you wasting another moment here with me when you could be with her?"

"She has to work."

She sighed. "Work always gets in the way, doesn't it?"

"I'm sure you could stay home if you really wanted to."

"Sometimes," she said. "But I really love being inside this bakery. I couldn't imagine doing anything else."

"Yo, the coolest guy in the world is here." Axel walked inside wearing a suit and tie. A wedding ring was on his left hand, but other than that, he looked the same.

I grinned from ear-to-ear when I saw him. He and I were pretty close when I was dating Francesca. I knew he was rooting for us despite his friendship with Hawke. "Look who it is."

"Kyle?" he asked in surprise. "What are you doing here?" He gave me a quick embrace.

"Just talking to Francesca about my love life." It didn't sound weird in my head but now that I said it out loud it didn't really make any sense.

"Really?" Kyle asked in surprise.

"She's actually been very helpful."

"The woman who was on and off with Hawke for four years?" Axel asked incredulously.

"You're one to talk," Francesca snapped. "I understand women pretty well and I was giving Kyle some help. And I think that help paid off."

Axel shook his head and looked at me. "Don't listen to anything that woman says. It's a guaranteed death sentence."

She grabbed a handful of powder and prepared to throw it at him.

"This is Armani." Axel held up his hand and took a step back.

Francesca still had a mischievous grin on her face.

"Throw that and you'll have to find a new babysitter for Suzie," Axel warned. "I'm not bluffing."

"Oh whatever," Francesca said as she returned the powder to the bag. "You love her just as much as your kids."

Axel tried to keep a straight face. "That's not the point."

I actually missed the banter between them. I didn't realize that until then.

"Why are you here?" Francesca asked.

"Just wanted to stop by and say hi." Axel returned his hands to his pockets when the threat passed.

Francesca rolled her eyes. "You just want me to make you lunch."

"I never said that," Axel argued.

"But you do," Francesca snapped.

"Okay...maybe I do." Axel shrugged in guilt.

"I don't even make lunch for Hawke," Francesca said.

"No wonder why he's so grouchy all the time," Axel said. "Everything is coming together."

Francesca rolled her eyes again then ignored him. "You want anything, Kyle?"

"No, it's okay. I should get going anyway. Just wanted to thank you for what you did."

"No problem," she said. "Hawke and I are here if you need anything."

"So, Hawke knows Kyle is here?" Axel asked in surprise.

"Yes," Francesca said. "Hawke likes him."

Both of his eyebrows were raised. "Does he not remember who Kyle is...?"

"He's matured," Francesca said. "The past is in the past."

"I don't know about that," Axel said. "If some guy was hanging around Marie, I'd kill him."

"No, you wouldn't," Francesca argued.

I knew another argument was just around the corner so I should get out of there. "I'll give you an update on how things are going."

"Thanks," Francesca said. "And I hope Rose will still work on Hawke's office. He really likes what she's done with the place, even if you'd made her change things just to stall."

"Great," I said. "I'll let her know."

***

The second I finished up my paperwork at the office, I texted Rose. *Can I take you out to dinner?*

As long as there's dessert.

There always is.

I showered and got ready before I picked her up. Since we'd already dated I picked a more casual restaurant. I liked Indian food and so did she, so we went to a place just a few blocks from my place.

Dressed in a black dress, she looked beautiful like always. She curled her hair and pulled it over one shoulder, exposing the opposite one. She picked at the naan and dipped it in the hummus.

We didn't say much at dinner, but not because we were awkward. We spent most of the time just staring at each other, getting used to the fact we were in the same room. I spent most of my nights alone, and when I did go out to eat I didn't pay any attention to the person I was with.

She took a few small bites then glanced up at me to see my expression. Then she turned her gaze down again, acclimating to my relentless gawking. "How was your day?"

"Good. Yours?"

"I worked on a mountain house. It was pretty cool. When there's no other houses around there are more things I can do with the place."

"Cool." I was interested in her words, but not as much as her appearance. It was difficult to fathom that she was truly there—across from me. I thought our relationship was truly over—which was why I went out with Lea. "Made any progress on my house?"

"I made the changes you asked for. You should come by the office and I'll show you sometime."

"That sounds good." Anytime I got to see her, I was excited.

She ate another piece of naan then glanced at me. "You aren't eating."

I hadn't even taken a drink of my water. All I'd been doing was staring at her—pretty much gawking. "Just distracted..." I grabbed a piece and tried to act normal, eating and drinking like everyone else. Knowing she was more than just a girlfriend changed things. She was destined to be with me, as crazy as that sounded. And that kind of knowledge couldn't make me care less about what we ate or what restaurant we should go to. It was irrelevant.

We got through the rest of the meal in almost complete silence. Anytime she looked up I was looking at her, and the rare times I looked away her eyes were on me. A conversation passed between us—void of any words. But that seemed perfectly natural to the two of us.

I was eager to make love again but I could tell she wasn't ready for that. My need wasn't a physical one. Even though I hadn't had sex in months and I was going through a dry spell, I didn't want sex just for sex. I wanted that passionate, burning love we had once before. We only made love a handful of times before we went our separate ways, so I didn't have that experience with her enough times to be satisfied. If anything, it was just a big tease.

I wasn't sure exactly why she wasn't ready to be with me again. The trial may have opened old wounds, or maybe she still didn't completely trust me after keeping the truth from her.

I really didn't know.

But I wouldn't pressure her into something she wasn't ready for—no matter how much I may want it. She was my forever, and waiting a little longer wasn't much to ask for.

We finished dinner then walked to my apartment since it was closer than hers. Her apartment was just as nice but not quite as big. I had two bathrooms, so when girls brought their hair and makeup stuff they had a designated area to put it. Otherwise, my counter would be covered with eye shadow and hair spray.

We entered my apartment and turned on all the lights. It was suddenly clear how alone we were. It was just she and I—in an apartment that contained a bed. Sex was on my mind a lot because I was immensely attracted to her—and madly in love. It would be impossible not to feel that way with a woman like Rose. But I tried to pretend that static wasn't in the air. I tried to pretend my sex drive was non-existent. "Can I get you anything? Water?"

"Sure." She tucked her hair behind her ear then sat on the couch.

I retrieved it for her then took a seat beside her. "Let's see what's on..." I grabbed the remote and flipped through the channels until I found our favorite TV show. My arm casually moved to the back of the couch and felt the back of her neck. Like I hoped, her hand moved to my thigh.

I wanted to go straight to the bedroom and make out, making up for all the time we lost. Kissing was something I only did in the beginning of a relationship. As it progressed it disappeared. But I enjoyed kissing Rose. There was something innately sexy about it.

But I controlled myself and pretended to be content with watching TV.

She laughed at the funny parts of the show and loosened up. By the end of the program she was more relaxed. "That dog was cute."

"All dogs are cute."

"Why don't you have one?"

I shrugged. "Not sure. I guess there's just not enough room for one. He needs a yard and stuff."

"Your beach house would be the perfect setting."

"When I settle down and move out there, I'll definitely get one. I'm thinking about a great dane or a bulldog."

"Both excellent choices."

"What about you?"

"What?" she asked.

"What kind of dog would you like?"

"Any kind."

"Really?" I asked with a chuckle. "You have no preference?"

"I love all dogs."

"So, if I got a pitbull, you'd be cool with it?"

"Why not?"

"Because they're ferocious dogs." Or did she not watch the news?

"That's unfair. A lot of their owners train them to be that way. They have a label, and society continues that label by treating them that way."

"I never thought about it that way."

"If you got a baby pit bull and raised it with love, I'm sure he'd be fine."

"Even so, I'm going to stick with something else."

She finished her water and left the glass on the table. Her legs were crossed and her hair was still pulled over one shoulder. The skin was enticing and I wanted to lick the area, tasting every inch of her. She glanced at me and saw the look in my eyes. It was too quick for me to change my appearance. She knew. "I love you and I'm so glad we're back together but—"

"It's fine." We didn't need to have this conversation.

"What's fine?"

"If you aren't ready to be together again, I'm okay with that. Really." It took a long time to get her into bed the first time. It may take even longer this time. But she was the woman I was meant to be with, and I'd wait as long as she wanted. I wouldn't go looking for action anywhere else. Besides, sex with anyone else would be terrible. It would never be as good as it was with her.

She turned to me with remorseful eyes. "It's just...after the trial everything came flooding back and I can't get it out of my head." She closed her eyes like she was trying to keep the image away.

"Sweetheart, I understand." My hand moved to the back of her neck and I gently massaged her.

"It's nothing against you…"

"I know."

"It may just take me some time."

My hand moved to her chin and I turned her face in my direction. I patiently waited for her to open her eyes. When she finally did, there was fear deep in her eyes. "I'll wait as long as you want." My thumb rested in the corner of her mouth and I held myself back from kissing her.

"Now that you know everything, I'm afraid that's all you'll think about."

"I didn't think about it the first time." It didn't cross my mind at all. All I thought about was the woman I'd fallen for. "I see you for you and nothing else. Those men took something that didn't belong to them, but they didn't take all of you. You're just as perfect and beautiful as you were before that night. That's not what I think about when I look at you—I promise."

Her hand wrapped around my wrist and her thumb gently massaged my forearm. The hesitation was in her eyes, like she didn't believe me.

I wish she would. "You're mine. There was nothing before and there will be nothing after." All the women in my life stopped existing when she walked through the door. It was hard to believe I ever loved Francesca because that love is nothing compared to what I feel for Rose. To me, nothing was in Rose's life before I arrived. When you find the right person to spend your life with, everything in the past becomes irrelevant. It's as if it never happened at all.

**

I made dinner for Rose at my place. It wasn't anything fancy, just grilled fish and rice. My cooking abilities were pretty limited so all I knew how to make was chicken and fish.

"This is really good." Rose finished her plate then wiped her lips with a napkin.

"Thanks. It's one of the few things I know how to make."

"Well, you know me. I can only make a bowl of cereal."

"And it's a delicious bowl of cereal." I cleared the plates and set them in the sink to wash later. I was the kind of guy that let the dishes build up until a dangerous level before I finally washed them. The sink was pretty big so I had plenty of time to procrastinate. "What do you want to do?"

She blanched like the question was intrusive. "We could watch a movie."

I'd been waiting for her to loosen up physically, but nothing seemed to have changed. I was a patient man, but I wanted her so much it was difficult to be patient. "Sure." We moved to the couch and turned on the TV.

She pulled a blanket over her lap and cuddled into my side.

A week ago, we made out in my bedroom, completely naked. I wanted to do that again. There was no release at the end but it was still enjoyable. Being connected to her like that was the most intoxicating experience of my life.

I turned to her, my lips dangerously close to hers.

She glanced at my lips then looked away.

My hand slid up her cheek and dug into her hair. When I looked at her, I saw a beautiful woman who was even more beautiful underneath. My fingers found a good grip in her hair and I leaned in, slowly making the descent.

She flinched slightly, unprepared for the kiss.

I kissed her slowly, finally feeling our lips touch. They were soft like always and glided across my skin. The familiar taste of vanilla flooded my senses. The moment we touched I fell even deeper. I got lost in those kisses, drunk off her touch and scent.

I wanted to kiss her forever—just like this. I sucked her bottom lip and heard the small gasp she released. I wanted her to feel as good as I did, so I gave her my best moves. When I kissed Lea, all I thought about was Rose. The kiss was forced and bland. But with Rose every kiss was magical.

Rose abruptly pulled away. "Sorry…" She touched her bottom lip like she'd been bit.

My hand slowly left her hair, unsure what happened.

"I just…I don't know."

When she came back into my life, I assumed her walls were still down. But now they were back up like she never trusted me to begin with. I was understanding but still disappointed. "Sweetheart, what's wrong?"

"I'm not ready to be physical yet. I'm sorry."

"Not even kissing?" She was fine the other night. Why was it any different now?

"Kissing is fine. I just don't want it to lead anywhere else."

"That's fine. Whatever you want."

She didn't give me her lips. Her walls were still up.

"Sweetheart?"

"I'm just afraid if we start something up it'll head down that road…"

Again, I tried not to be offended. If it were a different situation, I might be frustrated. But I could never begin to understand what she went through. I read every police report, every testimony, and I saw all the evidence. What happened to her wasn't just rape. It was traumatizing just to read about. She deserved all the patience she asked for. But I didn't want her to hide away from everything in fear. I wanted her to take steps forward. "I have an idea."

"An idea?" she asked in surprise.

"Yeah. Come with me." I walked into the bedroom and opened my nightstand.

She stood behind me, her arms across her chest.

I pulled out the handcuffs and the key. "Let's give these a try."

Both of her eyebrows rose to the ceiling.

"Let me explain." I didn't want her to jump to some ridiculous conclusion. "The police force gave this to me as a gift when I was the prosecutor on their case. One of their officers had been killed in the line of duty, and I got justice for his family. Anyway, I think we can use these."

"I don't think so…"

"Let me show you." I kicked off my shoes then lay back on the bed. My bed had metal bars as the headboard so I cuffed myself to it with the key sitting on the pillow beside me. "These are real." I yanked on the headboard. "I can't get away unless you uncuff me."

She continued to look as confused as ever.

"Climb on top of me."

She didn't make a move.

"You can kiss me all you want without worrying where it'll go. I can't do anything if I'm chained up like this. You have all the power." Power was something she never had before. She was always at the mercy of others—but now she wouldn't be.

Her arms slowly lowered to her sides. "I appreciate the thought but you shouldn't have to be chained up like a criminal. I trust you, Kyle. This is unnecessary."

"But it'll make you more comfortable. It's not forever and it's just a start. Besides, I think it's kind of sexy." I yanked on the cuffs to make them rattle. "I feel like a prisoner at your mercy."

"You're sure?"

"Absolutely." I directed her with a nod. "Now come here."

She crawled on top of me and positioned herself. Her hair hung down, just inches from my shoulder. The hesitation was still in her eyes, like she was unsure if this was a good idea or not.

I thrust my hips up slightly. "Come on. My lips are getting cold."

She finally smiled before she leaned in and pressed her mouth to mine.

The second I felt her lips I lost all my playfulness. I melted into her like always and reveled at the way our mouths moved together. Our chemistry was so perfect that it was volatile. It could explode at any moment. I wish she would let me in completely. If she did, we would have some really amazing sex.

After a few moments, she really got into it. She touched me more than she usually did, feeling my chest and stomach. Her hips were in line with mine, and if she moved the right way she could feel my hard-on in my jeans. There were times when I automatically yanked on the cuffs because I wanted to touch her, but the clank of the metal reminded me I was stuck.

It became more heated as time went on and I thought my dick would explode because I was so hot for her. How I would survive the forthcoming weeks without sex was beyond me. Jerking off wasn't an option because that was just weird—when I had a girlfriend. I'd have to stick it out and keep my mind focused on other things.

But that was impossible at the moment.

Rose pulled away then sat upright, straddling my hips as well as my hard dick.

I didn't want the session to end. I loved kissing her. It was better than any sex I'd ever had.

Then she did the unexpected. She pulled her shirt over her head.

I stiffened in place, seeing the flawless skin of her stomach and chest. Every curve was highlighted despite the darkness of my bedroom, and somehow I became harder at the sight.

Damn.

She unclasped her bra and let that fall on my thighs. Her firm and round tits were delectable. I remembered the way each one felt in my mouth. Her nipples were hard and pebbled. Now I wanted to run my tongue over them and suck them until they were raw.

What was she doing to me?

She leaned down and pulled my shirt up to my shoulders, revealing my bare chest and chiseled stomach. Then she kissed me again, her naked torso pressed against mine.

It felt so good it hurt.

I yanked on the chains again, desperate to touch her. The metal cut into my wrists but the pain was irrelevant. I didn't even feel it.

I kissed her hard, wanting her more than I'd ever had. She was so sexy and she didn't even realize it. When I looked at her and felt her, it seemed like I was the only person who'd been allowed to do such things. I wish she could see herself as the beautiful and perfect woman she was. No one could take her purity away from her—not unless she gave it away. "You're so beautiful it hurts."

She paused in our embrace, her lips still touching mine. Then her hand migrated up my chest to the area just over my heart. "As are you."

***

I held Suzie in a single arm at the table. She looked just like her mother but had her father's formidable eyes. Dark strands of hair protruded from her forehead, and she had the cutest smile I'd ever seen.

Francesca took advantage of my offer to hold her daughter so she could eat her burger and fries.

"Hawke isn't coming?" We were sitting inside Mega Shake, my favorite place to eat. Francesca had never been there before, so I suggested we meet there.

"He has to meet with a client today."

"Oh. On a Sunday?"

"With Hawke's business, he works all the time."

"Does that mean he's not home often?" With a new baby in the picture that didn't seem fair.

"He comes home every night and he spends time with us, but sometimes he has a client that can only meet at a certain time, like the weekend. Believe me, he hates it when that happens." She picked at a few fries then turned her attention to Suzie in my arms. A small smile crept across her lips.

"And he's okay with...this?"

"With what?" she asked blankly.

"You and I hanging out alone."

"He doesn't care in the least. I already said that."

"But we were at your bakery. Now we're hanging out as friends."

"Trust me, he doesn't care."

I don't think I'd ever be okay with Rose hanging out with an ex, even if we were married. In fact, it would bother me more. "So, he knows I'm here with you."

"And our daughter."

This would take me a long time to understand. "So, if he hung out with an old girlfriend, you'd be okay with it?"

"He doesn't have any old girlfriends, just flings. So no, it wouldn't bother me. But those situations aren't the same. You aren't into me anymore, Kyle. You have someone in your life."

"I suppose." Hawke used to be extremely territorial. He may be nice now, but I'll never forget the feud we had. We were about to rip each other's throats out.

"So, how's it going with Rose? If you're having lunch with me, it must not be perfect."

"It could be better."

"What's wrong?"

I moved Suzie to a different arm then leaned back in the booth. She was so small, almost as light as a feather. It was hard to believe she would grow up into a person someday. "Rose is pretty...hesitant." It was the best way I could describe it.

"Hesitant?"

"She's not ready to be physical yet."

"But you've already slept together."

"I know, but the trial changed things. She's not the same."

"Oh..." Francesca swirled her fry in her ketchup but didn't take a bite. "I'm sorry. I can't even imagine..."

"I understand how she feels. I probably understand better than anyone since I was the attorney on the case. But I wish she would trust me and understand what we have is nothing like her previous experience. And I want her to know I don't think about that stuff when I'm with her."

"She thinks all you think about is what happened?"

I nodded. "But I don't. Honestly." Actually, I put it far, far into the back of my mind. It was too difficult to think about. Every day of the trial I wanted to throw up in the bathroom. "She doesn't deserve to be looked at like some kind of charity case, damaged goods. And I don't look at her that way."

"Maybe you need to remind her."

"I have. And believe me, I show it." I kissed her with passion and gripped her so tightly she could never leave my embrace. "I guess I'll just have to wait until she comes to terms with it on her own."

"Maybe she should see a therapist."

I shrugged.

"Has she ever done that?"

"Not that I know of."

"It couldn't hurt. You could go with her."

"I guess that's not a bad idea. But honestly, I'm not sure if I want to hear her talk about it. Upsets me..."

"Show her that you can handle it. Maybe when she sees how supportive you are, she'll let her walls come down."

"Maybe." But could I handle hearing her talk about how painful that night was? So far, I'd only heard objective recollections of that crime. I looked at the evidence and the police reports. I'd never heard Rose speak of it herself.

And that was completely different.

"I wish she would understand I'm her soul mate. Maybe if she did, all of her problems would go away."

"Maybe you need to tell her."

"No. I want her to figure it out on her own." If she did, I would never be scared of losing her. I would trust her completely. And I would no longer be scared of letting her slip from my grasp.

"That may take some time."

Sunday

"Well, I'm not going anywhere."

***

"Hey, sweetheart." I walked inside her office and approached her desk.

"Hey." Her face lit up the moment she saw me. She practically jumped to her feet just to hug me.

I missed that.

I kissed her forehead then rested my chin on her head. "Excited to see me?"

"Always."

I rubbed her back and melted into her, never wanting to leave this embrace. Being close to her like this was exactly what I craved—every hour of every day.

"What brings you here?" She pulled away from my chest and gave me a quick kiss on the lips. She hesitated at the end, as if she wanted to keep kissing me but was unsure if she should.

She always should.

"I just wanted to check on your plans for the house."

"Sure." She opened her cabinet and pulled out the folder that contained the drawings. "I made all the changes you asked for." She rolled out the print across the desk so we could both take a look at it.

I sat across from her and eyed it. She did exactly what I asked, bringing my vision to life. "It looks great."

"Thanks. Do you have any other changes?"

I searched my mind as I examined the drawing. "Do you have any recommendations?"

"Recommendations?" she asked.

"Yeah. If this were your home, what would you do?" I lifted my gaze and searched her eyes.

"Uh...I don't know."

"Not a thing?" I asked in surprise.

"Well, if it were my house, I'd probably have a separate sitting room. You know, with just elegant furniture, a fireplace, and a great view of the ocean."

"You mean a living room?"

"No. This room wouldn't have a TV. It would be a quiet place dedicated to reading and conversation. You know, when you have people over for tea and stuff like that."

"Like in the 1800's?" I teased.

She ignored the jab. "I love TV as much as the next person, but it would be nice to have a quiet place to read and enjoy other people's company. I don't know...it's something I've always wanted."

I nodded in agreement. "When you put it like that it's intriguing. How about we add that in?"

"Why?" she asked. "I'll have to redo the floor plan with the game room."

"The game room can be smaller. I don't even play that many games."

"But you play more games than sit by the fire and read."

"Maybe I'll give it a try if it's there."

She stared at me quizzically. "Are you sure that's what you want? I'll make the changes but are you sure you want to do it?"

"Absolutely." There wasn't a doubt in my mind.

When she saw the confidence, she turned to her notepad and wrote it down.

"Any other suggestions?"

"This is your house, Kyle. My suggestions are irrelevant."

"Come on," I pressed. "I want your opinion. You do this for a living. You probably have a lot of insight."

"Well..." She rested the pen against her bottom lip. "I think a walk-in closet is essential."

"But there already is one."

"I mean a big walk-in closet."

The one I had wasn't big enough?

"I know you don't have a lot of clothes now, but over time possessions really pile up. I've never had a client complain about their walk-in closet. It's so much easier to put all of your stuff inside and walk in when you need something. The dressers in the bedroom are good for your undergarments and lay around clothes, stuff you don't mind getting wrinkled. But it keeps the room tidy when you have a completely separate place to put your things."

"Like another bedroom."

"Exactly."

I would never need that much space, but if that's something she wanted it would happen. "Then let's do it."

"Really?" she asked in surprise.

"Yeah."

Instead of doubting me again she wrote it down.

"What else?"

"If we keep doing this, we'll completely redo your house."

"That's fine with me. I'd rather get it right."

"Well, you only have one fireplace right now. You should have one in the bedroom and the other living room."

"Why?"

"It gets pretty cold in the winter. Fireplaces are so warm and inviting. They are just comfortable. I wish I could have one in my apartment."

"Then let's put them in."

She made the notes without objection.

"Anything else?"

"Uh, I think that's it."

"So, would you say this is your dream home?"

She shrugged. "I guess. But it's not my house."

"But hypothetically, would it be?" I watched her face closely.

"I'd say so. Anyone would die to live here. This place will be a masterpiece once it's finished."

That was good enough for me. "Great."

***

She walked inside my apartment with a tray of cookies. "I know you aren't much of a sweet tooth but I thought they were cute."

They were cookies cut into the shape of dinosaurs. White frosting outlined their bone structure so they looked like tiny fossils. "They are cute."

She smiled and set them down. "I made them from scratch."

"Even cuter." I grabbed her by the back of the neck and pulled her in for a kiss. I lived for these embraces. They were so sexy and innocent at the same time. Her lips were somehow softer than last time, and I had to stop myself from devouring her.

She pulled away before things became too heated. "How are you?"

"Good now that you're here."

She smiled beautifully, a look I never took for granted. "I'm glad to be here too."

I wanted to head into the bedroom and handcuff myself again but I had something more pressing to do. "There's something I want to talk to you about."

"Yeah?"

"I hope you keep an open mind to it." Whenever I brought this up she usually took off. Her natural reaction was to run—all the time. But she needed to stop doing that and face the music.

"Okay..."

"You and I should go see a therapist. You know, to talk about what happened that night. I think it would be good for you."

All of the joy that was on her face just a moment ago disappeared. "Why? What will that accomplish?"

"You obviously haven't moved on from it, and maybe talking to someone will help you get through it. I'm more than happy to be there too—if it helps."

The blood ran from her face, and now her cheeks were pale.

"I'm not trying to open old wounds, but I think the original ones haven't healed yet. Maybe if you talk about it it'll help our relationship—"

"Is this just because I won't sleep with you?" With a snap of her fingers she turned on me. Now she was defensive—even angry.

"Of course not." I was hurt she would even think that. I tried to hide the pain on my face but I couldn't. "But I think it's holding you back from being happy. I don't think the wedge between us is from me not telling you the truth. I think it stems from your own insecurities. There's no shame in admitting you need help. Not at all."

"Just because you're the attorney on Audrey's case doesn't mean you understand how I feel."

"I never said I did. But I want to help you get through this."

"I am through it."

"That's a lie and we both know it."

She turned away, her eyes filling with rage.

"Sweetheart, I'm not trying to upset you."

"Well, you did."

"Would talking to a therapist really be that bad?"

"Talking about how a group of guys raped me? Yes, that would be bad."

I closed my eyes for a moment because her words stung. "I think if you talked about it to someone it would give you closure. And you would let me in."

She shook her head and stepped away.

"You can't deny this is affecting your relationship with me. I'm okay with not being physical, but I'm not okay with you assuming that I think poorly of you. I'm not okay with these men taking away your life. I want you to be free—to be happy."

"Just stop."

I took a deep breath and kept my anger back. Snapping at her wouldn't get me anywhere. "I'm only trying to help."

"Well, don't."

Now it was becoming harder to keep my mouth shut.

"I should just go..." She headed to the door.

I didn't stop her. Was this the end of our relationship—again? Was she walking out on me? It nearly killed me the first time she did it, and now she was doing it again so easily. I may love her but I could never trust her—not if she walked away again.

She walked out and shut the door behind her.

I stood in the same spot, feeling like shit. I didn't feel guilty for saying what I said. But I did feel terrible that she left. I knew she was going through a hard time, and rightfully so, but so was I. I'd fallen in love with someone who experienced something so terrible she may never recover. Taking on that kind of romance was more than challenging. It was emotionally crippling and exhausting. But I never gave up on her and it cut me that she gave up on me.

It broke my heart.

The door opened again and she appeared.

I couldn't hide my surprise that she came back. Did she forget something? Was she going to take back the cookies she stole?

She walked over to me then kissed me on the cheek. "I'll call you later."

I was frozen in place, shocked by her affection.

"I love you." She walked out without waiting for me to say it back.

That final parting changed everything. She wasn't leaving me again. She just needed space.

And I was grateful she made that clear.

CHAPTER THIRTEEN

The Struggle

Rose

I didn't want to talk about what happened.

As it was, I didn't even think about it.

I did everything I could to pretend it didn't happen at all. Sometimes that night would haunt me in my dreams. Sometimes it would creep into my thoughts during the day. And sometimes when Kyle and I became physical the memories would blur with my reality.

But no, I never talked about it.

The fact Kyle mentioned it unnerved me. It reminded me that I wasn't okay, that I needed help—just as everyone else said. I knew Kyle didn't want a physical relationship if I wasn't ready for one. But I knew he was anxious for something more than I was ready to give.

In the back of my mind, I knew he was right.

But I wasn't strong enough to face it, to talk about that terrible night. As a defense mechanism I put it in the back of my mind, locked away in a box where I couldn't reach. It was the only way I could walk the streets without looking over my shoulder.

We hadn't spoken in a week, and when I walked out of his apartment, I immediately regretted my actions. I didn't mean to leave him so coldly and I didn't want him to assume our relationship was over. Now that I've lost him once I didn't want to go through that heartbreak again—even if I was mad at him.

A week later I finally cooled off enough to walk into his office. His firm was just a few blocks from mine, and it was designed with both elegance and masculinity. Secretaries sat at their desks while lawyers were locked away in their offices. I knew exactly where Kyle's was because it was directly after the entrance.

His secretary didn't stop me from walking inside because she knew exactly who I was. Kyle was sitting behind his desk with his feet resting on the surface. He was doing something on his phone, probably playing a game.

"Hi..."

He looked up at the sound of my voice, and his eyes held their surprise. He quickly lowered his feet to the ground and tossed his phone on the surface. A mixture of hesitance and joy was on his face. But he didn't rise from his chair, something he would normally do. "Hey."

I walked further into the room, feeling more self-conscious by the second. I could see the disappointment in his eyes, the irritation from my previous behavior. "Are you busy?"

"Does it look like I'm busy?"

He was definitely mad. I took the seat across from his desk, my hands still clinging together in front of my waist.

He gave me the same ruthless stare.

"I'm sorry about last week."

"Sorry about what, exactly?"

"I know you were just trying to help and I flipped out..."

"You haven't called me in a week. I'd say you did more than just flipped out."

Kyle usually gave me the easy way out but he wasn't going to do that this time. "I know..."

"How are we supposed to move on if you won't let me in?" he demanded with narrowed eyes. "You clearly have issues about this subject and I think we should do something about it. You've been avoiding it for four years and look where that's got you."

"I know..."

"So, let me help you."

His aggression was backing me into a corner. "It's not so simple as just getting over it."

"I never said it was. But let's try something new."

I clutched my hands together.

Kyle still didn't baby me. He was just as ruthless as before. "Rose, you can do this. I know it's hard, but you can overcome it."

"I just don't want to talk about it..."

"Rip the bandage off. Sometimes you have to get worse before you get better. So far you've just been procrastinating."

"You have no idea how I feel, so please keep that in mind." I tried to control my voice and remain calm. "You never walk the streets and feel predator eyes fall on you. You never go to a party and have to check your drink three times before having a single sip. You never have to worry if the guy you've been set up with is a rapist. No man will ever understand what it's like to be a woman."

He hung his head low and broke eye contact for the first time. "No, I suppose I'll never fully understand as I've never been in a woman's shoes. But I can confidently say I understand better than most. I think you forget what I do for a living. I think you forget what happened to someone I loved very much." He looked back at me, the sadness in his eyes. "You and I can get through this together. Don't you think it's a strange coincidence we've suffered the same tragedy and then we're set up on a blind date? I don't know about you, but I don't believe in coincidences."

"Then what do you believe in?"

He held my gaze for nearly a minute before he spoke. "Not sure…"

I looked down at my hands.

"Just keep in mind what I've been through. I can help you. Helping you helps me."

"How so?"

"For one, I love you. And two, if my sister survived, I'd want someone to help her."

It was true. Sometimes I forgot what Kyle endured when his sister passed away. Her murder still affected his family. It was a tragedy they would never forget. Sometimes I got stuck in my own bubble and shut out the world, convincing myself no one would ever understand. And if they did, they would still judge me for what my body endured.

But I knew Kyle wasn't that way. He was the definition of good. He was a great man, the most compassionate and caring man I've ever known. "I'm so sorry for my behavior..." The sincerity entered my throat and burned slightly.

His eyes softened. "It's okay, sweetheart."

"I'll try going to a therapist. I want to get better. And I want our relationship to work."

He finally rose from the desk and walked around until he was sitting beside me. He took my hand and brushed his thumb across the top of my hand. "Our relationship will work. And I think talking to a professional will help. If you're okay with it, I'd like to be there."

It would be hard enough to say the truth out loud, but it would be harder for Kyle to listen to it. "I don't want to hurt you...it'll hurt you."

"I know it will," he whispered. "But we should go through this together. I'm here for you every step of the way." He squeezed my hand.

"Thank you. I don't know what I did to deserve you. I don't know how our paths crossed. I don't know how...we found each other. But I'm so grateful we have."

I searched his eyes, seeing the searing blue eyes that burned me when I looked deep into them.

He stared back at me, giving me a look I'd never seen before. His hand squeezed me a little more firmly, and the emotion in his eyes was blinding. He didn't blink for over a minute, just staring at me without speaking. "Maybe we'll find out someday."

***

Kyle sat beside me in the armchair and held my hand on my thigh. He wore a suit because he just got off work, and despite his calm exterior I knew he was raging inside.

Dr. Caroline sat behind her desk with a notepad on the desk. She was nice and friendly, but a little stern at the same time. She had glasses just like I pictured, and her mouth always slightly curved in a frown.

I couldn't believe I was sitting across from a therapist. Never in my life did I picture myself sitting in this chair. Before that horrible evening, I had a happy life. I was outgoing and fun. Sometimes I was the life of the party. I dated a lot of guys without worrying where it would go, and I was adventurous.

But those aspects died that night.

I was never the same after that moment. Even when months passed, I never got back on my feet. Friendships died because I became so distant. My contact with people died away as well. Florence was the only friend who stood by my side—because she was the only one who knew.

Dr. Caroline glanced at Kyle before she spoke. "You're comfortable with Kyle being here to listen?"

"Yes." I was dreading the conversation. I didn't want to go into the details of my past. Kyle already knew everything, but hearing it come from my mouth was a different story.

Dr. Caroline turned to him. "Kyle, you're ready to listen?"

"I am." He said it with a firm voice, but he was good at hiding his emotions in front of other people. It's one of the characteristics of being a lawyer.

Dr. Caroline turned back to me. "Where would you like to start?"

I shrugged. "I don't know."

"Start at the beginning."

"When we were on the date?" I asked hesitantly.

"Yes." Dr. Caroline readied her pen.

I glanced at Kyle and felt the nerves get to me.

He squeezed my hand again, giving me a gentle push. "You can do it, sweetheart."

I turned back to Dr. Caroline and let everything out.

**

By the end of the session, I was sobbing. Everything hurt just as it did on that night. Old wounds were ripped wide open, and I was bleeding all over the place. My chest ached because my lungs wouldn't work correctly.

Kyle kept his arm around me and consoled me every step of the way. Despite the pain on his face he never gave into his grief. He just sat beside me and gave me everything I needed.

When our time was up he kissed my forehead and wiped my tears away. "You did a good job today."

"Then why do I feel so terrible?" I sniffed and wiped my tears away with the back of my forearm.

"It's part of the healing process." Dr. Caroline came around her desk then shook my hand. "I look forward to seeing you next week. I think we're going to do great things here."

All I could do was nod.

Dr. Caroline shook Kyle's hand. "You're doing the right thing. Being patient and understanding is the best way to help those we love."

"My sister went through the same thing," Kyle said sadly. "But she was murdered as well. Rose and I have a lot in common."

"Oh, I see." Dr. Caroline dropped her hand and gave him a sad look. "It looks like you two are perfect for one another."

"I couldn't agree more." Kyle wrapped his arm around my waist and walked me out. He kept me close to his side and steered us in the right direction. "Would you like to go home?"

I nodded and sniffed again.

"Let's go." He walked me to my apartment, guiding the way since my head was bowed the entire time. I managed to stop crying but I knew my face was red and blotchy. I didn't want anyone to stare at me, to know I was upset.

We got inside my apartment and Kyle immediately grabbed a few tissues so I could wipe up my face. I turned away and cleaned up my make up as well as I could without a mirror. I felt like a wreck, like someone ran me over with a fire truck.

"You did a good job today. I'm proud of you." He stood behind me and wrapped his arms around my waist. It was as if he knew I didn't want him to see my face.

"Thanks..."

"Do you want me to leave?" Resignation was in his voice, as if he expected me to ask.

"No."

His arms flinched slightly. "What would you like to do?"

"I want to go to bed..." It wasn't even six in the evening but I didn't feel like living life at the moment. I walked into my bedroom and collapsed on the bed without taking off my clothes. I kicked the sheets back and got inside, enjoying the darkness of the bedroom.

Kyle kicked off his shoes and lay beside me. He spooned me from behind and wrapped his arm tightly around my waist. "If there's anything I can get you, let me know."

"I just want to sleep...and wake up to a new day."

"Do you mind if I join you?"

"No." I felt better when he was near. I was becoming more dependent on his presence than ever before. He was the gate to my happiness. He brought more joy than I ever realized. I needed him in my life, and not just now, but forever. "I don't want you to ever leave, Kyle."

He tightened his arm around me. "I won't."

Sunday

CHAPTER FOURTEEN

Recovery

Kyle

Francesca walked inside my apartment, wearing her work t-shirt and jeans. She was covered in spots of flour and sugar, and her hair was in a braid over one shoulder. "What's up?"

"Hey." I grabbed a beer from the fridge and handed it to her. "How was work?"

She waved away my offer. "I can't have alcohol right now—not when I'm breastfeeding."

"Oh sorry." I didn't know anything about babies, but that one was obvious. "Water?"

"Water works."

I handed her a glass then sat down at the table. "Where's Suzie?"

"Marie took her and the twins to the zoo. They aren't home yet."

"Isn't Suzie a little young to be going to the zoo?"

Francesca shrugged. "I know she likes being with her cousins no matter what they do."

"Do you miss her?"

"All the time," she said with a sigh. "It's strange. I used to be obsessed with the bakery, but when she came into my life, it slipped from the number one spot. Now the bakery is number three."

"What's number two?" I asked in surprise.

"Hawke."

"Oh yeah..." That was obvious. "Does he know you're here?"

She rolled her eyes. "I've told you at least ten times he doesn't care if we hang out."

"But you're at my apartment. Isn't that a little different?"

"You've been to my house."

"But I'm your ex." I still couldn't believe he really didn't care.

"Whatever," she said. "That was a long time ago."

Not that long ago. "I just don't want to get my ass kicked by a lunatic."

"You've been with Hawke. Does it seem like he cares?"

"No..."

"Then you can relax." She drank half the glass before she set it down. "What's going on with Rose? Does she know you're soul mates yet?"

"No...but I think she's getting there."

"Really?"

"Well, she started seeing a therapist."

Francesca nodded. "That's good. Hawke did that for a while. Really helped him through his pain."

"What pain?"

She hesitated, like she said too much. "He had some issues growing up and they carried on into adulthood. But that doesn't matter now. Keep going."

I didn't ask any questions because it didn't seem like she wanted to tell me anything. "She went to the first session last week and it was pretty difficult for her. Walked out crying."

"Poor girl."

"But I think it's the best thing for her. She never talks about that night, and maybe saying everything out loud will give her the closure she needs to move on."

"You're probably right."

Hearing the recollection gave me indigestion for days. I couldn't get the taste of vomit out of my mouth. Hearing that heartbreaking story and knowing it wasn't just a story, but the truth, was damaging. I loved Rose no matter what, but it still crippled me a little. "I'm not giving up on our relationship. If she can conquer this, I think we could really have what we should have."

"You're so sweet, Kyle."

"Not really."

"How can you say that?" she asked in surprise. "You're the most compassionate person I've ever met."

"That's not true either," I said coldly. "I know she's my soul mate. That's why I haven't walked away. That's why I gave her another chance when she didn't deserve it. That's why I let her push me away and pull me back again. That's why I let her walk all over me."

"I can understand that—a lot."

I remembered the way Hawke pulled her back and forth. He would be there for a few months before he took off again. Francesca got emotional whiplash from it. "It sucks."

"Oh yeah."

"I know I have every right to walk away but I can't."

"Been there, done that." She finished her water and set the glass on the table.

"But I know she'll get through this and we'll have what we should have had from the beginning. I know she's strong. I know she'll pull through."

"And that belief will be enough."

"Yeah." I held my beer in my fingers and felt the coldness of the glass. It burned a little.

Sunday

Francesca's phone started to ring and she answered without checking to see whom it was. "Hey."

Hawke's voice came through the phone. "You aren't home."

"I'm still in the city."

"Where's my little girl?"

"She's still with Marie. She took the kids to the zoo."

"And when will my girls be back?"

"Forty-five minutes." She rubbed her finger along the rim of the glass.

"Where are you?"

"At Kyle's apartment."

Hawke didn't react at all. "Alright. You better be home in exactly forty-five minutes. There's no food on the table."

"You can feed yourself."

"But I prefer my Muffin's cooking."

Francesca's face softened but she didn't let the emotion leak over the phone. "Forty-five minutes."

"Forty-four." He hung up.

She chuckled then set the phone down. "Marriage..."

"You seem pretty happy to me."

"I am. But he's a bit of a caveman sometimes."

"I picked up on that..."

"Anyway." She crossed her arms on the table. "It sounds like things are going well with Rose, for the most part."

"It'll take us some time but we'll get there. Even in our darkest moments there's nowhere else I'd rather be."

She gave me a slight smile. "That's how you know you're in love."

***

I took Rose out to ice cream after work. The two of us split a sundae the size of Mount Rushmore.

"Can I have the cherry?" She pleaded with her eyes.

"Yes...because you're so cute."

She snatched it from the top and bit it off the stem. "Yum."

I got a scoop full of ice cream, whipped cream, and nuts. I didn't eat sweets very often, so when I did, the taste was overpowering. "This is really good."

"Ice cream is the best. The only thing it's missing is a hot brownie."

"Not your first rodeo, huh?" I asked with a smile.

"When it comes to ice cream, I know what I'm doing." Her leg moved under the table until it was resting against mine.

I loved it when she touched me. It didn't matter how. I loved any kind of affection. "Maybe your shop should be half an architect studio and half an ice cream parlor."

She laughed and almost spit out her ice cream. "That would be the weirdest business ever."

"Or would it?"

She chuckled and kept eating. "I don't think there would be a lot of cross promoting going on."

"You won't know until you try." I noticed her improved mood. It'd been a week since we went to see Dr. Caroline but she'd been doing well. She had a skip in her step and she was a lot more playful than before. Perhaps talking about everything with a professional was really helping after all.

She finished her half of the ice cream then licked the chocolate sauce from her fingertips. "Thanks for the ice cream."

"Anything my lady wants, she gets."

She gave me that usual pretty smile.

"Is there anything else you'd like to do?"

"No, I'm pretty full. I think I'm ready to turn in."

I'd been sleeping at her place every night and I wanted to keep up that tradition. Even though most of my bed was taken up by a woman, she hogged the blankets, and her alarm woke me up, it was still better than sleeping alone. I loved having her right beside me. "Let's go."

We left the parlor and walked down the block. "How about we stay at your place?"

It didn't make a difference to me. "Sure." I grabbed her hand and held it as we walked.

Sunday

She moved in further and wrapped her arm through mine, hooking me tightly.

I couldn't keep the smile off my face.

We entered my apartment then went straight into the bedroom. That's where Rose went so I followed. It was too early to go to sleep but perhaps she wanted to lay together and cuddle.

Just when I kicked off my shoes, she opened my nightstand drawer. I'd never seen her go through my things before, and now I wasn't sure why she was doing it. I had nothing to hide but I didn't appreciate someone snooping. "Do you need something?"

She pulled out the pair of handcuffs we used once before. "Can we use these tonight?"

My dick hardened at the thought. "Sure."

She pulled my shirt over my head before she guided me to the bed. Like last time she cuffed me to the headboard so I couldn't get anywhere. Then she did something she'd never done before. She removed my jeans and boxers before she pulled off my socks.

I was completely naked—and cuffed.

242

And I liked it.

She crawled on top of me then kissed my chest. Her tongue moved across the grooves of my pectoral muscles until she slowly crept up my jaw. She sprinkled kisses everywhere until she found the corner of my mouth. A slow kiss was placed on my lips, so slow it was actually painful.

This was hot.

She held herself on top of me as she kissed me ferociously. Her slow kisses became heated and hot. She sucked my bottom lip before she gave me a bit of her tongue.

I got goosebumps.

Then she abruptly left my lips and slowly trickled down my body to my stomach. She kissed the valleys indented in the muscle before she moved even lower, past my hips.

And my cock twitched.

Her lips moved to the base of my dick and she kissed the area, her tongue rubbing against my balls.

Oh shit.

She worked her mouth around the base, licking and kissing. Then she grabbed my dick and pointed it upwards, allowing her to lick my balls then suck them deep into her mouth.

I yanked so hard on the cuffs I almost broke the headboard.

She licked her wet tongue up my base, moving right over a vein, and then licked the top of it, sucking in some of the pre-cum I let escape. She opened her mouth wide before she took me into her throat, and she took in as much as she could while massaging my balls with her soft fingers.

Hot damn.

I yanked on the cuffs again, desperate to dig my hands into her hair. I hated being held back, forced to keep my hands to myself. I wanted to be there in this moment, to feel the soft skin between her shoulder blades.

But this was the most progress we ever had. She was doing something innately sexual to me—and more importantly—she liked it. She was still uneasy if my hands were tied back, but it was better than nothing.

And I really enjoyed it.

She pumped my dick with her hand while she licked the head, waiting for me to squirt in the back of her throat.

I hadn't gotten any action in so long I couldn't remember the last time. My dick was high on the feeling and I couldn't control my body. Everything she was doing felt so amazing. It was the best head I'd ever gotten— hands down. "Sweetheart, I'm about to come." The polite thing to do was warn her of what was about to happen.

She gave me a sexy look with my dick still in her mouth. "Then come."

I pulled on the cuffs and felt the explosion start at my base. Everything was propelled down my shaft before it burst from the end. It filled her completely, giving her more seed than I'd ever produced in my life.

And it felt so damn good.

"Rose..." I felt lightheaded from the explosion and I slowly drifted down to earth, feeling my heart finally slow down. My entire body felt tender from the pleasure, and the exhaustion crept in afterwards.

She spread kisses on my stomach and chest before she met me at the headboard. She grabbed the key and unlocked me, allowing my hands to come free.

I immediately grabbed her and pulled her to my chest. "What was that for?"

"What do you mean?"

"Why did you do that?"

"I wanted to. What other reason would there be?"

"I just don't want you to do things just for me..."

"I didn't." She kissed the corner of my mouth before she crawled off of me. "Believe me, I like having your dick in my mouth."

My cock twitched all over again.

***

"Dude, you'll never guess what happened." I walked into the back of the bakery talking a million miles an hour. "Rose handcuffed me to the bed last night and gave me the best head I've ever—" I stopped when I spotted Hawke in the background with Suzie in his arms.

246

He was sitting down, so Francesca's frame blocked him a moment before. "Uh, never mind."

Francesca chuckled at the embarrassed look on my face. "She's only a few months old. She doesn't understand what you're saying."

"Still weird...she's a baby."

Hawke sat up with Suzie still cradled in his arm. "What's up, man?"

"Nothing..." I still felt awkward around him and I suspected I always would. I just walked into his wife's bakery like I had every right. "You?"

"Marie is sick so I took Suzie to work today," Hawke explained. "We just stopped by for lunch."

"Muffins, specifically," Francesca said with a smile.

"Well, I should get going..." I started to back up. "I'll talk to you later."

"Hold on." Hawke handed Suzie over before he walked up to me.

I knew it. He was pissed I was spending time with Francesca. And he had every right to feel that way. He married her. I didn't.

"Frankie tells me you're afraid you're pissing me off by hanging around her." He crossed his arms over his chest, looking threatening.

"Sometimes I worry about it."

"Honestly, I don't care. You don't need to walk on eggshells anymore. There's nothing wrong with the two of you being friends."

He was definitely a bigger man than I was. If I were the one who married Francesca, I wouldn't want her anywhere near him. "Are you sure?"

"Absolutely," he said. "I know you don't feel that way about her anymore. So there's no harm."

Hawke wouldn't lie about something like this. If he were ticked, he'd make it clear. "Well, thank you."

He clapped me on the shoulder. "Now, get back over here and tell us about your girl problems."

"Okay," I said with a chuckle.

"So, you got some action last night?" Francesca asked as she handed Suzie back to Hawke. She returned to making frosting from scratch.

E. L. Todd

"Yeah." I smiled just from thinking about it. "Such good head. It came out of nowhere. She just went ahead and did it."

"With you handcuffed?" Hawke asked. "That's pretty hot." He gave Francesca a knowing look, like he wanted her to do that to him later.

"It was definitely hot." There was no other way to describe it.

"And a little fast," Francesca said. "She went from being reserved to really hot and heavy action?"

"Well, the handcuffs are for a different reason, actually. She likes having them so she knows it can't go any further than she wants..." It was an awkward thing to say but it was the truth.

"Oh..." Francesca let the realization sink in. "Now I understand."

"But it's still an improvement for us. I think therapy is really getting her somewhere."

"That's great," Francesca said. "It's good to talk about things with an unbiased professional."

"I agree," I said. "Despite what I've been through, I can't give her what she needs. I'm not trained for it."

"It sounds like all you need to do is wait it out." Francesca whisked the frosting then poured it into a separate container. Hawke tried to stick his finger in it but she swatted him away.

"Yeah." Now that something physical happened between us, I knew we were headed in the right direction. Everything would be okay—in time.

"And pretty soon we can go on a double date," Francesca said. "And our kids can play with each other."

Hawke chuckled. "Baby, don't freak him out."

"I'm not," I said calmly. "There's nothing I want more than a wife and two kids." I eyed them with jealousy in my heart. Their relationship was a lot of work and a lot of heartache but they had something truly beautiful now. And I wanted it.

CHAPTER FIFTEEN

Deep Inside

Rose

I felt good after the last session with Dr. Caroline but now I dreaded the next one. I told her the whole story from beginning to end last time, and now I wasn't sure what else there was to say.

But I'm sure Dr. Caroline would find something.

When Kyle picked me up he noticed my sadness. "There's nothing to be afraid of."

"I'm not afraid." I may be timid and skittish but I was never scared.

"Then there's no need to be nervous."

"I just don't want to go." *Plain and simple.*

He took my hand and walked me out. "But I think it's been helpful. You've been different this week..."

I knew he was referring to the blowjob I gave him the other day. It was unexpected and I didn't even know it was coming, but when we were in his apartment I wanted to do something. Without thinking his clothes were off and my mouth was tight around his base.

I loved making him feel good, and I loved the fact it made me feel good too. I didn't think about that night four years ago. All I thought about was us. His hands were restrained so I knew he couldn't do anything I wasn't ready for. And perhaps that made me feel freer.

"I think I have been different."

"You seem happier, more at ease, and more adventurous..."

"Yeah, I noticed it too."

"So, I think this is a good thing." He wrapped his arm around my waist and kissed me on the temple.

"You're probably right."

We walked to the office downtown then entered Dr. Caroline's room. She had a beautiful office with floor-to-ceiling windows. It had a warmth to it, and it also didn't feel like a cage. It was open and inviting, like I could go and come whenever I pleased.

"It's nice to see you two again." Dr. Caroline was just as stiff as usual. She had a compassionate demeanor but she was also straight-down-to-business.

"You too," Kyle said for both of us.

"How was your week?" Dr. Caroline asked.

"Good," I answered. "Better than other weeks."

"Do you feel like our talk helped?" she asked.

"I did...although it was difficult at the time."

Dr. Caroline nodded in understanding. "Traumas like that are difficult to move on from...no matter how much time has passed. Talking about it in our last session seems to be helpful. But now I want to focus on the future."

What did that mean?

"I want to focus on your new relationship with Kyle. It's important not to allow new relationships to be affected by the past. It can be easy to do, and it seems to be something you're struggling with."

"Yes..."

"Trust is the most important aspect of a relationship. If it's not there, the relationship will never succeed. You need to ask yourself if you trust Kyle. You don't need to answer out loud but you need to think about it—"

"I do." Despite the way he lied to me I did trust him. I knew he was compassionate, caring, and devoted. He would never make me do something I wasn't comfortable with, and he always had my best interest at heart. "I do."

Kyle squeezed my thigh affectionately.

"He's been amazing since the beginning. I tried to keep him away for a long time, afraid of what he would think of me after what happened, but I could never shake him off. Months passed and somehow...I fell in love with him. I never told him what happened to me because I was scared it would chase him away. Little did I know he already knew everything...because he represented a client in a case against my same attacker. He didn't tell me this before we slept together because he wanted to wait until the trial was over. I was so humiliated that I pushed him away for months...and then I asked him to take me back because I couldn't live without him." I told her our entire story, rambling on longer than I should have.

Dr. Caroline spun her pen in her fingertips for several minutes, her eyes looking at me but not really seeing me. "Kyle, could you give us a moment, please?"

"Of course." He squeezed my thigh before he walked out.

When he was gone, I turned back to Dr. Caroline, unsure why she asked him to leave. "I didn't just say that because he was sitting there." I meant every word.

"I believe you." She returned to spinning her pen. "You speak so highly of him, so why are you afraid to further your relationship?"

"I'm not sure...I guess I'm afraid things will never get better. That I'll remember being raped when I make love to him. That I'll attribute those feelings to Kyle and begin to resent him. That he'll only see me as damaged goods. That he'll think about the disgusting things that were done to me by other men..."

"You've had intercourse with him before, right?"

"Yes." *And it was beautiful.*

"Did you think about all of those things then?"

"Well, no. But that was different."

"How so?"

"At the time, I assumed he didn't know anything."

"But he did, right?"

I nodded.

"And did it seem like that's what he was thinking about?"

I shook my head. "Not at all."

"From my observations, it seems like the two of you have a lot in common."

There was no denying that.

"His devotion to you is fueled by the loss of his sister. Perhaps protecting you and loving you makes him feel better about what happened. It redeems him from not saving his sister when he could have. Defending you and another victim in the case was heroic. And the fact he's the one who brings you here and supports you so strongly tells me he doesn't think less of you. In fact, he thinks the world of you."

I knew that—deep in my heart.

"In my professional opinion, two broken people don't make a good relationship. Positivity needs to come from both partners for the relationship to work. But in your case, it works. I think trusting Kyle is a good decision, and I think he deserves the same devotion he gives to you."

"I know..." I would always feel guilty for the way I hurt him.

"Your priority should be this relationship. You need to connect, heal, and grow. When you do, I can assure you that both of you will be better. I think the two of you need each other to move on."

That was becoming more evident with every passing day. "I think you're right."

She nodded. "Make it happen, Rose."

***

"If you don't mind me asking, what did the two of you talk about?" Kyle took off his jacket and hung it over of the back of the chair at the kitchen table.

"Mainly about you."

"Yeah?" he asked. "I hope good things were said."

"She told me to focus on our relationship. We're better together than apart."

"I couldn't agree more." He slid his arms around my waist then pressed his lips into my hairline. He held me that way for a long time, for minutes. One hand snaked up to my neck where he gently massaged it while his lips were still pressed against me.

"That was about it..." There was more to it but I lost my train of thought when he held me this way.

"I'm glad these sessions are helping. That's what I hoped for."

"Me too."

He moved his face near mine and looked into my eyes, the longing and desire written all over his face. He glanced at my lips, wanting to kiss me.

I wanted to kiss him too but I immediately thought of the anxiety and the fear.

Kyle immediately noticed it. "You can trust me."

I wanted to grab the handcuffs, the metal that kept him restrained during our heated moments, but I wanted this relationship to reach its full potential. I wanted us to have what we needed. "Okay."

He slowly backed me up into the kitchen cabinets then lifted me from the ground and placed me on the surface. My legs dangled to the floor and he moved between my knees, our faces level. Normally, he towered over me and had to crane his neck just to reach my lips. But when we were like this, it was perfect.

Kyle found my lips with his and kissed me slowly, in a purposeful way. He studied my lips with his, feeling every inch as if he was going to memorize it. His hands moved to my thighs and he squeezed them affectionately.

My body lit up a few degrees.

His kisses migrated to my neck and he kissed me with the same slowness.

My head rolled back and I just enjoyed it. My nipples were hard as knives and they chaffed against my bra. But I was too turned on to care.

His hands slowly slid up my thighs and underneath my shirt. They glided until they reached the bottom of my bra. He fingered it slowly, feeling the lace.

Then he moved underneath and felt my tits, squeezing them and massaging them.

It felt so good.

His mouth returned to mine and they moved together with heated precision. His tongue entered my mouth and slowly moved against mine. They were dancing, touching.

I felt my panties soak from the moisture he elicited, and now I wanted to feel that familiar stretching sensation. I wanted to feel him inside me just the way I used to. We didn't make love enough times for me to truly treasure it. But I didn't make a move for it because I wasn't sure if I was ready. And if I wasn't sure, then I probably wasn't.

"You know what?" He rubbed his nose against mine.

"Hmm?" I just wanted to go back to kissing as soon as possible.

"I think my favorite thing to do is kiss you."

"More than the other things we do?" I thought I gave him pretty good head the other day.

"No. More than anything." He rubbed his nose against mine again before he returned to kissing me on the countertop. His large hands continued to rub me gently, and he made my entire body come alive. "I love you more than anything."

***

I stared at the different selection of lingerie and couldn't figure out what to do. Some were slutty and others were super slutty...which was appropriate for me? I wanted to dress up for Kyle so we could move on in our relationships, but looking at the black lace just gave me anxiety. It was too sexy, and I was anything but sexy. I couldn't pull off the look. I wasn't even comfortable in my own skin.

"Can I help you with something?" the saleswoman asked.

"Uh, no." I shook my head dramatically.

"Is this your first time shopping for lingerie?"

Was it embarrassing that my answer was yes? "Yeah...but I didn't see anything I liked so I'm just going to go."

The saleswoman had no intention of letting me walk away. "Let me pick out a few things for you. What bra size are you? 34B?"

I automatically touched my chest. "Uh, yeah."

"Hold on and let me fetch you something."

"Okay..."

She left for nearly five minutes before she came back with a black ensemble. It was a skin-tight teddy with garters and a black thong. A pair of shiny black heels was in her other hand. "What do you think?"

I shrugged. "I don't know. Do you think a guy would like that?"

"With your body, absolutely." She handed everything over. "Take these home. I promise you won't regret it."

I eyed the pile of slutty clothes in my hands.

"Trust me." She patted me on the hand before she walked away.

***

I stared at myself in the mirror. I wore the garters and the black stockings, and it took me nearly five minutes just to get into the teddy. I curled my hair and did my makeup darker than I'd ever done it in my life.

"I look like a slut."

When I looked in the mirror, I didn't see me at all. I saw some girl with big hair and dark eye makeup staring blankly at me. There was no way Kyle would think this is sexy. I looked like a woman that was trying too hard.

There was a knock on the door.

That must be Kyle. He said he was coming to bring dinner but I thought he wouldn't be there for another hour. "I'll be there in a second." I quickly kicked off my heels and tried to get the teddy off. It took a decade just to get it on so how would I get off?

Kyle walked inside with a plastic bag of food in his hand. My bedroom door was open so he looked right in, seeing me in my ridiculous lingerie. His hand slipped and he dropped the bag on the floor.

I slammed the door as quickly as possible, mortified that he saw me. "I told you to hold on."

"Sorry, I thought you said come in."

"Well, I didn't!" My fingers worked furiously on the back of the teddy, trying to unzip it and free myself.

Kyle opened my bedroom door and walked inside.

"What the hell are you doing?" I turned on him while trying to get the zipper undone.

"I just wanted to—"

"Get out!"

He raised both hands in the air in surrender. "You look like you need help."

"I'm fine," I hissed.

"Come here." He turned me around and unzipped the teddy halfway so it would still stay on but I could do it the rest of the way. "I don't want you to break your arms trying to bend that way."

"Thanks…" I waited for him to leave.

"You look hot, by the way."

"You're just saying that." I couldn't face him. I was too embarrassed.

"I'm really not." He grabbed my shoulders and turned me around slowly. Then he grabbed my hand and pressed it into his crotch. "Definitely not just saying that."

"I still look goofy as hell."

"Not in the least. But I admit you do look just as good in other things."

"Like what?" I had no idea what he talking about.

He opened one of my drawers and pulled out one of his t-shirts. "Nothing beats a boyfriend's shirt." He tossed it on the bed beside me. "And it's cheaper than the fortune you spent on that."

"The girl at the store talked me into buying it..."

"I really like it. But maybe we should use it some other time...down the road."

"Yeah?"

He cupped my face and forced my look on him. "I want you—just you. I don't want some hot supermodel look alike. I want you just as yourself, with no makeup, a baggy t-shirt, and that look of love in your eyes. That gets me hot like nothing else."

"I thought if I dressed like this we could power through and you wouldn't think about—"

"I don't want to power through. If anything, I want to slow down. And I don't think about anything but you anyway. When will you start believing that?"

I looked down because I didn't have an answer.

He pressed a quick kiss to my neck. "Change. I'll try to salvage the dinner." He walked out and shut the door behind him.

Feeling just as embarrassed as before, I changed into the oversized t-shirt and washed the make up from my face. He said I looked sexy, which increased my confidence, but he also knew I was trying too hard. In the event of trying to push this relationship forward I may have pushed it back.

***

When Kyle dropped the bag he spilled the food everywhere and it couldn't be saved. So we ordered a pizza instead. It wasn't as delicious as the Chinese food we originally ordered, but it would do.

Kyle draped his arm over the couch and gently rubbed the back of my neck. "All of the attorneys at my office are booked up with cases so I may have to take on some clients."

"You can't just turn them away?"

"I feel weird doing that. If they come to us for legal help, we should be there. But I've never been in this situation before, where all my attorneys aren't available."

"Maybe you should hire more people?"

"I think I may have to. But I hate the process...all the interviews and resumes." He pointed a fake gun to his head and pulled the trigger. "So much reading and they all say the same bullshit."

"Why don't you have someone else do it?"

"I like to know who I'm paying. So I have to do it."

"In Manhattan there are probably some pretty good applicants."

"Like, a million," Kyle said. "And that's the problem."

I snuggled into his side and wrapped my arm around his hard waist. The empty pizza box sat on the table, only the crumbs left behind. *America's Funniest*

Home Videos was on the TV but I wasn't paying attention to it. "I love the way you smell."

"Strange compliment, but I'll take it." He kissed my forehead and kept watching TV.

"It makes me feel good. I can't explain it."

"No, I know what you mean."

I looked up into his face and saw him looking down at me. After enough hours passed my confidence had returned after the lingerie incident. Now I wanted to feel him, just like we did in the kitchen the other day.

I sucked up my courage and straddled his hips, my hair falling down my shoulders and toward his face.

His hands immediately went to my thighs, where they normally rested.

My hands slowly guided up his chest until I reached his shoulders. The muscles of his body always got me aroused. I loved how fit and strong he was. I loved his natural power and strength. He had the body of a warrior but the heart of a child.

Within a minute, I felt his hard-on form underneath me. It was like a tree log poking me in the inner thigh. The touch aroused me even more. Even when I felt the least sexy, he found me attractive.

I pressed my chest to his and kissed him slowly. The TV was loud in the background, the audience laughing at a video with a cat in it. Without breaking our embrace, Kyle turned down the volume with the remote and continued to kiss me. His hand returned to my thigh a moment later, gently feeling me.

My hands dug into his hair as I deepened our kiss, and I felt the ecstasy all over my body. I was hot and cold at the same time, feeling everything a person could feel at one time.

His hands moved to my hips then my stomach, gripping me tightly. His hips rocked slightly, his hard-on rubbing against me through his jeans.

Our kiss went on for nearly thirty minutes until I reached a new point of arousal. My body was burning hot and desperate for more than just his kiss. I wanted to go further tonight, finally make love and move on with our lives. I was so turned on that I knew it could happen. "Let's go in my room."

Kyle left the couch with my body wrapped around his. With perfect ease he carried me into his bedroom and placed me on the mattress. His body immediately covered mine and he kissed me with more excitement.

My hands worked his clothes, removing his jeans and his shirt. I stripped him down until he was naked, hot and hard. He did the same to me, getting me down to my panties before he removed those too.

I wrapped my legs around his waist then grabbed his dick and pointed it at my entrance, telling him I was ready for something more than just kissing.

But instead of sliding inside he pulled his hips away.

"I think I'm ready."

He placed a kiss between the valley of my breasts before he looked me in the eye. "Don't rush it."

"I'm not—"

"You are." He dug one hand into my hair. "This isn't something you can just rush and get through. It doesn't work like that."

Then when would I be ready?

He answered my unspoken question. "I'll know."

"How?" He knew me better than anyone but he still couldn't read my mind.

"Trust me. I'll just know."

"I don't think that's something you can just detect."

"Not for anyone else. But for me, I can. Just relax and be yourself. When the time is right, I'll handle everything."

It was a strange thing to say, but I knew I needed to start trusting him. I had the greatest guy in the world right in front of me, and I needed to appreciate him more. "Okay."

When I finally agreed he smiled. "Thank you." He scooted down and widened my legs, his lips immediately moving to mine. His tongue did something amazing to my clitoris and I immediately dug my nails into the sheets.

"Oh god…" My back naturally arched and I held back the scream.

"I've wanted to do this for a long time."

And now I wanted him to do it for a *long time*. "Kyle..."

He pressed his face further into me and did amazing things. All I could understand was how good it felt. Everything else faded into the background. My hands moved from the sheets to his forearms, and I dug my nails into his skin. I knew what was about to happen and my body was never prepared for it. It was a crescendo of sensations, and it rocked me every single time.

Kyle moved up my body until we were face-to-face. His hand moved to my clitoris and he rubbed it aggressively, looking me in the eye as he did it. Then he kissed me slowly, the taste of myself on his lips.

The feel of his lips against mine and the aggressive way he touched me sent me over the edge. I felt my body tighten painfully before the blissful release. I'd been so hard up from all the kissing we did, and now my entire being was grateful for the explosion. It seemed to go on forever because Kyle dragged it out as long as possible. His fingers continued to work my clitoris, and even when my mouth widened to scream, he still kissed me in the most seductive way imaginable.

"Oh god..." When the orgasm passed, my nails stopped cutting into his forearms and I felt logic descend. I looked into his eyes knowing my face was still slack and unexpressive.

The desire was still heavy on his face, like he got his own kick from watching my show. "You're beautiful when you come."

Instantly, my cheeks reddened. I knew he'd been watching me, but at the moment I didn't care. Now I did. I became self-conscious and a bit doubtful.

"It was hot." My legs were still open to him so he grabbed my hips and shifted me against him before he pulled the covers over us.

"What are you doing?"

"Getting ready for bed."

I wasn't the kind of girl to be selfish in bed. It'd been a long time since I had a physical relationship but I knew that, at least. I pulled the covers down again and moved toward him.

He grabbed my shoulder and gently guided me back against the mattress. "I'm fine. I'm paying you back for that little performance you did last week."

"You're still hard."

"I'm always hard around you." He set the alarm on my nightstand then turned off the light. "So, that doesn't mean anything." He cuddled into me, his large arms wrapping around me like bent cages.

"Well...thank you."

He chuckled. "You're welcome. But you don't need to thank me. Believe me, I enjoyed it."

"No. I mean, thank you for being so patient and understanding..." No other guy would put up with my issues. They'd all leave the second they knew the truth. Kyle was a hero in my eyes.

His face softened immediately. "I'd wait forever for you, sweetheart."

"I'll never understand why you love me so much."

His fingers glided through my hair slowly and pulled the strands from my face. The concentrated expression told me he was about to say something. Even

274

his lips parted. But then they abruptly closed again and he fell silent. His fingers trailed across my cheek and his thumb rested in the corner of my mouth. "One day you will."

Sunday

CHAPTER SIXTEEN

Babysitting

Kyle

I was sitting at home during the day when I got an unexpected call from Hawke.

"Hey. Are you ready to go over the plans for the new office?"

He barked into the phone. "Busy right now?"

"Uh, I'm at home. Why?"

A crying baby sounded in the background. "Axel is in California for a conference, Marie is sick, and I have a really important meeting to get to. Can I drop off Suzie for a few hours?"

Here? With me? "I've got to be honest. I don't know anything about kids."

"That's fine. Just make sure she doesn't get hurt for two hours."

"Uh…"

"Are you going to help me out or what?"

"What about Frankie?"

"She's in the middle of making a wedding cake. She can't handle Suzie right now."

Was I the only option? "You don't have any other friends?"

"Why are you being a dick right now?" he asked. "Is Frankie your friend or what? You go to her every week for advice and help with Rose. You're really going to leave us hanging?"

When he put it like that, I did feel like an ass. "I don't mind helping you. I just don't have any experience with kids. Are you sure you want to leave your newborn baby with me? Some guy?"

"You aren't some guy," he growled into the phone. "And is that a yes?"

It was only for two hours. I could handle that, right? "Yeah."

"I'll be there in five minutes."

***

Hawke set the car seat on the ground with Suzie inside of it, and handed me the backpack full of diapers, bottles, and toys. "I'll be back in two hours."

"What do I do with her?" I eyed her in the car seat. She was kicking her feet slightly with a smile on her face.

"She's not an alien," he snapped. "Just sit with her. Play with her."

"What if she's hungry?"

"Surely, you know how to give her a bottle."

"What if she poops?"

"Change her diaper."

"Do I look like I know how to do that?"

"Have you heard of YouTube?" He eyed his watch. "Look, I've got to go. Call me if you have a problem—not Frankie." He kneeled down and gave his daughter a kiss. His voice completely changed when he spoke to her. "Daddy will be right back. Love you."

She reached out with her small hand and grabbed his nose.

Hawke chuckled then kissed her small fingers. "Uncle Kyle will take good care of you." He rose to his feet and headed to the door. "Good luck."

"Thanks." I watched him go then redirected my eyes to Suzie.

She stared at me blankly, like she had no idea who I was.

"So…"

The same blank stare.

"Are you hungry or anything?"

She kicked her feet.

"Um, what do you want to do?"

She farted.

I tried not to laugh. "Well, let's watch TV." I picked up the car seat and placed it on the coffee table. I turned the car seat so she faced me and I started watching TV again.

She stared at me and giggled from time-to-time.

"Babies aren't too hard..." They just sat there quietly. When she wasn't crying it was pretty nice. And if I were lucky enough she wouldn't poop or pee so I didn't have to change her diaper. My house would reek for a week.

Someone knocked on the door.

Was it Hawke? "Who's there?"

"It's me." Rose opened the door with a bag of take-out on her arm. "I thought I'd bring your lunch."

My life lit up like it always did when she walked in. "Free food and free service? This is starting to be a pretty good day."

She smiled then set the food on the table. That's when she noticed Suzie. "Uh...who's this?"

"Oh." I turned back to Suzie and gave her foot a gentle pinch. "This is Suzie."

"And who does she belong to...?"

"She's Hawke and Francesca's daughter." I carried Suzie to the kitchen and placed her on the table. "Hawke asked me to watch her for a few hours."

Rose looked into the car seat and smiled. "Awe. She's so cute."

"I know."

She peered her head inside then gently tickled Suzie's stomach. "Adorable."

"She's quiet too. Haven't heard a peep from her since she arrived."

"I'm sure that will change," she said with a chuckle.

"I'm glad you're here. Now you can babysit her."

"Whoa, hold on." She turned to me and raised her finger. "They asked *you* to watch her, not me."

"But since you're here you may as well take over." I wrapped my arm around her waist and gave her a kiss.

Like always, she melted and forgot about our argument.

"So, what did you bring me?"

"Sandwiches."

"Awesome. You're the perfect girlfriend."

"Because I bring you food?" she asked incredulously.

"Let me explain something to you. Men are very easy to understand. As long as you keep them fed, they'll be happy and stick around."

"How romantic…"

I shrugged in guilt. "It's the truth." I sat down with my food and began to eat.

She took the seat beside me and took a few bites of her vegetarian sandwich while looking at Suzie. "I didn't realize you were so close to Hawke and Frankie—enough to babysit."

"I'm not. Hawke said he had nowhere else to take her. His sister-in-law is sick, and Frankie is busy."

"They don't have family?" she asked.

"Well, I don't think Hawke does. Not sure. He never talks about it. I know Francesca's grandmother is around but since she got remarried she's been doing a lot of traveling."

"What about Francesca's parents?"

I shook my head in response.

Rose caught onto my meaning and remained silent. "Well, since you agreed once, they'll probably ask you again."

"If she's cute and quiet like this, I don't mind."

"You'll have to change her diaper eventually."

"That's what you're here for, woman."

She threw a chip at me. "You're lucky I know you're joking."

"Or am I?" I wiggled my eyebrows.

She threw another chip at me.

"Keep it up and you won't be getting any action from me," I warned.

"Is that really a threat?" she asked with a laugh.

"Yep. My face won't be between your legs."

She rolled her eyes but didn't throw another chip at me. And that told me everything I needed to know.

***

Rose changed Suzie's diaper and cleaned her up. "That wasn't so bad."

I grabbed the dirty diaper by the very tip then shoved into a plastic bag. I tied up the ends into an unbreakable knot before I threw it in my garbage. I was breathing through my mouth the entire time. "Yuck."

"Your mom changed your diaper. I bet it wasn't yuck then."

"Of course not. My poop smelled good."

She rolled her eyes. "I'm sure." She fixed Suzie's clothes before she returned her to the car seat.

I came back into the living room and sat on the floor beside Rose. "I'll need you on baby duty if I have to watch her again."

"What will you do when you have kids?" she asked. "Just let the woman do it?"

I didn't like the way she spoke of our future. She acted like there was a possibility that I would be married to someone else, have kids with someone else. Rose was the woman I was going to marry. Did she not feel the same way? Was she not there yet? "I can tell you'll be a great mother. I won't have to do anything."

She turned to me, surprise and anger on her face. "Yes, you will have to do things. And I'm going to let that comment go because of what you said right before."

"And what was that?"

"That you want me to be the mother of your children..."

"No. You *will* be the mother of my children." I had that faith, that foresight. Unfortunately, she didn't. Hopefully one day she'll have the same belief.

***

"How was she?" The second the door was open, Hawke headed into the living room and picked up Suzie from the car seat. He held her in his arms and against his chest with his eyes directed on her exclusively. Wearing a black suit and tie, he looked like an enormous giant with a tiny baby. "Sorry Daddy was gone for so long." He rocked her slightly and held her tiny hand in his.

"Oh my god," Rose whispered. "That's the cutest thing I've ever seen."

"What?"

"How much he loves his daughter."

"All dads love their daughters."

"But he's so stern and stiff all the time. It's cute that he's not like that with her."

"I guess." I still didn't see it.

Hawke returned Suzie to the car seat then packed up her things. "Does she need a diaper change?"

"Rose took care of it," I answered.

Hawke carried Suzie's car seat back to the door. "She's a keeper, Kyle."

"I know." *But I already knew that.*

"Thanks for watching her," Hawke said.

"Anytime." I said that too quickly. "Anytime Rose is here. I don't exactly understand babies just yet."

"Whatever," Rose said. "Kyle was great with her."

Hawke shook my hand. "You really helped me out today. If you need anything, let me know."

"I'm pretty sure I'm paying you back for the favor you already gave me."

He chuckled. "I guess so. Are you guys doing anything tonight?"

Probably just full around. "Nothing exciting. What about you?"

"Francesca and I don't have any plans. How about the four of us have dinner?"

Hawke just asked me on a double date? "For real?"

"Yes," he said with a smirk. "For real."

"Uh...sure." I spent time with Francesca all the time. All four of us being together shouldn't be weird.

"That'd be great," Rose said. "We could see Suzie more."

"I'll talk to my wife and let you know." He walked out with Suzie on his arm. "See ya."

"See ya." I waved then shut the door.

"He's such a good father," Rose said. "He's so sweet."

"He used to be a goblin."

"A what?" she blurted.

"When Frankie and I were dating, he was a nightmare. We were close to ripping each other's heads off."

"It looks like you got over that."

"Thankfully." Now that time seemed like a lifetime ago.

"I think it's nice that the three of you can be friends. Not many exes can do that."

The only reason why Francesca and I started talking again was because of Rose, but she didn't need to know that. "We're both in such different places now. She's happily married, and I'm happy with you."

"I think it's great."

"So, what should we do before dinner?" I asked.

She shrugged. "What do you want to do?"

I wanted to make out and get naked—what I always wanted to do. "Let's watch a movie."

"Okay."

Sunday

CHAPTER SEVENTEEN

Dinner

Rose

Francesca spent most of her time looking down at Suzie beside her chair. She was in the car seat and tucked under a blanket, plastic keys in her hand. Hawke would do the same, leaning over to check on their daughter.

I thought it was cute.

Kyle moved his hand to my thigh and rested it there while he looked at the menu. "I think I'm going to get the spaghetti. You know, stick with a classic."

Hawke eyed the selections. "I think I'm going to have a spring salad."

Francesca didn't bother hiding her annoyance. She rolled her eyes dramatically than sipped her water.

Without looking at her once, Hawke knew what she just did. "I saw that."

"Who orders salad at dinner?" Francesca asked. "If anyone should be ordering a salad, it's me. I have baby weight to lose."

Now Hawke rolled his eyes. "Whatever, Muffin."

"You have, like, seven percent body fat," she argued. "Order the lasagna."

"I'll order the lasagna if you order the salad—and we switch," Hawke said.

I'd never witnessed any of their conversations like this, and it was interesting to see how they behaved with each other. They were argumentative but romantic at the same time.

"Hell no," Francesca said. "I'm ordering the cheesiest and greasiest piece of lasagna—and you are too."

Hawke made eye contact with Kyle and shook his head slightly. "You dodged a bullet, man."

"I can see that," he said with a laugh.

"I'm getting the tour de France," I said. "It comes with a little bit of everything."

Kyle gave me a genuine smile, clearly happy I wasn't doing the salad dance. "Excellent choice, sweetheart." He squeezed my thigh gently under the table.

Francesca kept her eyes on Suzie, holding up a toy so she could play with it.

Hawke eyed her and cleared his throat. "If she's okay, let's get back to dinner."

Francesca turned to him with fire in her eyes. "I'm sorry. Do you want me to ignore our daughter?"

"I just think you should leave her alone for five minutes." He said it calmly but knew something bad was coming.

Kyle looked at me and lowered his voice. "I'm glad we don't argue like that."

I pressed my lips tightly together and tried not to laugh.

Francesca had fire in her eyes but she kept the flames back. "Fine."

"Great." He poured himself another glass of wine. "This is a great wine, Rose. Thanks for choosing it."

"Sure," I said.

Kyle changed the subject before things could get too heated. "I hired three more attorneys for my office."

"Really?" Francesca asked in interest. "That's a lot of people."

"Business has really picked up recently," Kyle explained. "I'm not sure why. I don't want to take on any cases unless I want to, so I had to do it."

"Because it would interfere with your golfing time?" Francesca teased.

"And my girlfriend time." He squeezed my thigh again.

"That's a smart way to go about it," Hawke said. "I hope I have that kind of privilege someday."

"You don't control your own hours now?" I asked.

"I do but I'm not done growing," Hawke said. "I want the business to be in a strong place so I can step aside if I wish. Right now, there's too much going on. I don't trust anyone to run the company besides myself."

"I feel the same way," Francesca said.

"I just realized something," I said. "We're all business owners."

Kyle slowly raised an eyebrow. "Wow. You're right. Never noticed that before." He held up his glass of wine to make a toast. "To running the show." He clanked his glass against everyone else's, including Francesca's glass of water.

The waiter arrived shortly afterward and took our order. Like I expected, Hawke ended up ordering the lasagna. Even when he stood up to her, he always let her win. That was something I noticed from the beginning.

"How are things going with you two?" Francesca asked.

"Great," I said. "We just went to Coney Island the other day."

"Awe," Francesca said. "That must have been fun."

"It was." Kyle took me around to do all sorts of fun things. He never made any physical moves toward me besides kissing and other things. But he never tried to make love to me. He said he would know when I was ready, but I wasn't sure how he would know that exactly. But his confidence stopped me from asking further questions.

"I miss going on dates and stuff," Francesca said. "Now that Suzie is here it's all work and married life."

"We still have a pretty romantic life together." A slight tone of defense was in Hawke's voice.

"Of course we do," Francesca said. "But we don't stay locked up in our bedroom all day anymore. Now we have another person to concentrate on."

"When I came home yesterday, I brought flowers," Hawke reminded her.

"I know," Francesca said. "I remember."

"Well, make sure you tell people I'm the most romantic husband in the world—because I am." He grabbed a piece of bread from the basket and took a few bites.

Francesca looked at Kyle then rolled her eyes. "Even soul mates can be annoying…"

"Soul mates?" I blurted. The words came out without thinking. I should have held my tongue as well as my incredulity.

"Hawke and I are soul mates." Francesca said it with complete seriousness. "We knew the moment we met, and we still know to this day. So, it's okay if he gives me a hard time about things. Because, at the end of the day it doesn't change anything. I'll tell him to order lasagna every time we go out and he may or may not do it. But when everything is said and done that truth is still there."

I'd never heard anyone say something like that, except in TV and movies. I considered myself to be a skeptic of that sort of thing. I didn't believe in destiny or in soul mates. After what happened to me I hardly believed in humanity.

But I believed her.

I'd seen them together, their interactions as well as the love that burned in their eyes constantly. When she took a step, he immediately reacted in an equal and opposite way. Hawke treasured both Francesca and Suzie like they were the most precious things in the world, and only the belief in destiny would stop Hawke from being threatened by Kyle—who dated Francesca. If I didn't see this first hand, I would write her off as a hopeless romantic.

But I could see it in them.

"That's sweet," I said. "I've never heard anyone say that before."

"It's extremely rare. Honestly, if I hadn't experienced it myself, I'd consider it to be crap. But when Hawke came into my life...I knew." She looked down at her daughter for a moment before she turned back to me. "When you meet him, you just know. There's not a specific reason or explanation. It is what it is."

Somehow, in a strange way, I knew exactly what she was talking about. I was suddenly more aware of the way Kyle gripped my thigh. His fingers were placed on me firmly, and anytime I moved, he moved with me. I remembered all the times when Kyle knew what I was thinking when I hadn't said a word. I remembered everything he did for me when he found out the truth of my past. And I remembered the way he took on the case just to make sure my attacker was put behind bars forever. Our paths crossed in many different ways. I didn't realize how strange that was until now.

***

"They are cute together."

Kyle held my hand as we walked back to his apartment.

"Yeah, I guess."

"Do you think of her as your ex-girlfriend?"

"Not really," he said. "I'm not sure how to explain it. I guess I see her as a really good friend. When we were together we had a good friendship as well as a romantic relationship. When we broke up I missed the friendship more than anything else. It's nice to have that again."

"They both seem like really good people."

"They are—even Hawke."

"He seems like someone who's had a difficult life."

"He has," Kyle said. "I don't know what that entails because Francesca never told me, but I know there's more to it."

"At least he seems happy now."

"When you find the right person all the pain seems to slip away." He brushed his thumb over mine as he focused on our path straight ahead. His other hand was in his pocket. "So, have you worked on my dream house?"

"Yeah, I made all the changes."

"Great. Now it's time to build it."

"Are you sure you're ready for that?" He took a lot of my suggestions when he didn't have the very same ideas to begin with. Sometimes I wasn't sure if it was what he really wanted—or what I wanted.

"Why wouldn't I be? We've been working on that house for a long time."

"It's just...do you really want the walk-in closet and the sitting room?" They were classic things that I would want. But would he want them? A feeling deep inside me told me those suggestions weren't in his self-interest. But why would he lie?

"Absolutely."

"But you don't have a ton of clothes. And you don't sit around much unless you're playing a game—which would require a TV."

"Well, I'm not going to live in that house alone forever." He pulled me down the block toward his apartment. I wasn't paying attention to where we were going, but he knew his way around.

"But how can you know someone else will like it?"'

He looked down at me, a faraway look in his eyes. "Because you told me you liked all of those things."

My heart skipped a beat, and then skipped another beat. For a second I thought I was dead because my body suddenly shut down. His words sunk into my skin for several seconds. The meaning wasn't clear at first, but as time passed the truth rang like a loud bell.

"My wife has to love the place too. She needs some kind of compensation for putting up with my bullshit all the time." He gave me a playful smirk, clearly loving the floored reaction I just gave.

"So, when you spoke of your future wife you were—"

"Referring to you. I'm surprised it took you so long to figure that out on your own." He squeezed my hand and kept walking like this conversation wasn't as serious as it actually was.

"I'm so lucky I found you." The words left my lips quicker than I could stop them. Lately, I blurted things out without thinking, but maybe that wasn't such a bad idea.

He looked down at me again. "I'm lucky I found you too."

"But you've put me back together. You've brought me back to life."

"And you think you haven't done the same for me?" He stopped in the middle of the sidewalk. The night was quiet and there wasn't much traffic around. It suddenly fell silent.

"It just seems like I'm the one we're always concentrating on..."

"You don't understand how much satisfaction I got for putting that piece-of-shit in jail. Knowing he'll never do this to another woman gives me some form of happiness. I wish someone put my sister's attacker in jail before he got to her. It doesn't bring her back, but I know she'd be proud of me for saving as many women as I can. You do put me back together, Rose. This is just as therapeutic for me as it is for you."

Unsure what to say, I just stared at him. A million feelings hit me at once, and now I didn't know how to process everything I was feeling. "Don't you think it's strange that we've been through the same thing, and then we just run into each other on a blind date?"

He tilted his head slightly. "No. I don't think it's strange at all."

"It almost seems like our paths were meant to cross." I knew I sounded crazy but that didn't stop me from saying it.

"Perhaps they were." He gave me the hardest look I'd ever received. He bore so hard into my face that he could see everything inside me. He could see my soul, my heart, and everything else.

The stare was too much, too powerful, so I looked away. Even with my gaze averted I could feel his hot stare.

He looked at me like he expected more, expected me to say something else.

***

We lay together in the shade of a beech tree in the park. The sun filtered through the leaves and filled the area around us with distinct warmth. Our depleted lunch sat in a plastic bag off to the side.

Kyle stared up at the sky, watching the leaves sway in the slight breeze. His hand was in mine and his ankles were crossed. "I wish it was spring all year round. In the wintertime, the snow is annoying. And in the summer, it's way too humid."

"I like spring too."

"Plus, the tourists aren't here yet."

"They do love to visit."

He moved one hand underneath his head, this thumb still rubbing against mine on the grass.

"How's your mom?"

"Good. She's still getting used to the change."

"Of being married?"

"Yes. And living at his place."

"Does that mean the mansion is empty?"

"Yeah."

"Is she going to sell it? Rent it out?"

"I doubt it," he said. "She's too close to that place. I suspect she'll just leave it there."

"Sounds like a waste."

"Since she and my dad lived there for most of their lives, it'll be too painful for her to sell it. I suspect she'll give it to me."

"That would be generous."

"Then I would give it to my kids someday. Wouldn't be able to sell it either."

Kyle and I were broken up for a while, and since he was close to his mom, I assumed he told her. "I'm guessing she doesn't like me as much as she used to…"

"Why do you say that?"

"Because I left you." My eyes were glued to the canopy so I wouldn't have to look at him.

His voice came out quiet. "I never told her."

"Really?" That was music to my ears. His mom seemed to hate Francesca with every fiber of her being. I didn't want to be next on her shit list.

"I always hoped we'd get back together. I didn't want to tell her unless there was absolutely no possibility of us making it work."

"That's a relief."

He turned on his side and propped up his head on his palm. He looked down at me, those crystal blue eyes more memorizing than the ocean. "Why?"

"I didn't want her to hate me."

"My mom would never hate you."

"She doesn't seem to be a big fan of Francesca."

"Well...as much as I care about Francesca, she deserves it. But you, no."

How could he say that when I hurt him so much?

"You had every right to walk away. I should have told you the truth from the beginning. My mom would never think less of you for that."

I swallowed the lump in my throat. "Does that mean she knows?"

"No." He assured me with his eyes. "I would never tell anyone unless I had your explicit permission."

I sighed in relief. The last thing I wanted was for people to know. It was humiliating and destructive. No one would ever look at me the same. They would just see me as a victim that couldn't recover. "I don't want you to tell her."

"I assumed," he said. "But I hope you change your mind someday."

"Why would I want her to know?" That would be awkward.

"Well, she lost a daughter in a similar way. If anything, I think you may help her in the way you helped me."

My eyes turned away.

"You're too hard on yourself. No one would think less of you."

"You're the only one who doesn't look at me like that. But everyone else does."

He grinned from ear-to-ear.

It wasn't exactly something to smile about. I gave him a look of confusion, unsure where his sudden jolt of joy came from. We were just discussing the night I was raped. What could be good about that? "What?"

"You said I don't look at you like that."

I hadn't paid attention to anything I said. I'd been doing that a lot more lately.

"That makes me happy. Finally, you believe me."

I did believe him. He always looked at me with nothing but love in his eyes. Sometimes he would graze his fingers down my cheek until they rested on my bottom lip. He wanted me in a physical way, but he also adored me like something that was innocent and pure. Now that I'd finally begun to put the past behind me, I started to notice all the subtle things. I thought about that night less and less. Slowly, I was starting to not think about it at all. "I guess it just took me a while."

"That's fine. We both know I was never in a hurry." His hand dug into my hair until his fingers wrapped around the back of my neck. He pulled my face to his and gave me a sweet kiss under the trees. It was slow and purposeful, and full of everlasting love.

I kissed the man I loved and knew he loved me too.

***

The alarm went off, loud and screeching.

Kyle hit the button and silenced it before it split our skulls. He sat up and pinched the bridge of his nose, unable to wake up with the rest of the world. He was shirtless and just in his boxers.

I didn't want him to go. I wanted him to lay with me all through the morning. When his body was wrapped around mine, I was never cold. His strong muscles acted as a natural heater, and his skin was delicious on my tongue. I didn't have to be in the office today, and now I wished he didn't have to go to work. "Stay with me." I rested his hand on his arm.

His voice was raspy from just waking up. "It's payday. I have to give out the checks."

"Right this second? Is the bank even open?"

"I've got to do all the paperwork and talk to my accountant."

I pouted my lips because I was growing desperate. Anytime he was away from me I felt like I was drowning. He'd become a security blanket I loved to wear at all times. "Stay for a few more hours. It's way too early."

"Sweetheart, you're making this really hard for me."

"You're making it hard for *me*."

"I've never seen you like this before."

Neither had I. "It hurts when you're away. It's like a pain right on my heart."

He returned to the bed and rolled on top of me. "Right here?" He placed a soft kiss on the skin right over my heart.

"Yeah."

"Well, I can't allow my sweetheart to be in pain, can I?"

I shook my head and ran my hands up his chest. My legs automatically wrapped around his waist and I was instantly wet. My body yearned for his in a way it never had before. I wanted to feel him inside me, to make love in the softest and sweetest way possible. It was always on my mind, and the yearning drove me slightly insane. "Make love to me."

His skin immediately prickled under my fingertips, goosebumps erupting everywhere. He took an involuntary breath and couldn't keep the desire out of his eyes. "I will." Like always, one hand dug into my hair and he kissed me. "With my mouth."

Sunday

CHAPTER EIGHTEEN

The Wait

Kyle

Practicing abstinence was the hardest thing I've ever had to do. When Rose and I were just spending time together, I didn't struggle with my desires. She didn't want it, so I didn't want it either. But now that I knew she wanted me, had asked me to make love to her not once, but twice, I was losing my grip on sanity.

She was ready for me, and she seemed to be a different person. Her therapy sessions helped and she finally let me in. She finally trusted me in a way she never did before. It would probably be fine if we went all the way.

But I still wanted her to realize what we were to each other.

She'd hinted at it many times. She knew our paths crossed for a reason, and she understood it wasn't just a strange coincidence that we met on a blind date. But she still hadn't reached the final conclusion.

So I had to wait.

Thankfully, we did other stuff. We had hot and heavy make out sessions, and she deep-throated me like a pro. The amateur stuff was enjoyable, but I really wanted the grand finale. I'd made love to her before, but it'd been so long that I felt like this was the first time all over again.

"So, have you slid into home plate yet?" Francesca sat across from me eating a salad. She was in her work clothes with her hair pulled into a single braid.

"Not yet."

"Man, that's brutal. Hawke made me wait a few weeks one time...thought I was going to die."

That didn't sound like him. "Why would he make you wait?"

"He said he wanted it to be special." She rolled her eyes. "He was thinking about it too hard."

I didn't realize just how romantic he was until Francesca told me.

"What are you waiting for?"

"She hasn't realized the truth yet. I'm waiting for her to get there."

"Who knows how long that will take?"

"I don't think it'll be much longer. She's said a few things, like she thinks our paths were meant to cross and stuff like that...but she hasn't gotten to the end yet."

"She said that?"

I nodded. "After we had dinner with you guys. And she's been a lot more clingy with me. Whenever I have to leave, she asks me to stay. Whenever we're together, she wants me to sleep over. And even when we don't see each other, she wants me to sleep over."

"It sounds like it's exactly what you want."

"It is." I just wish I didn't have to hold back anymore.

"Are you nervous?"

"For?"

"You know...the deed."

"I've slept with her before."

"But this time it'll be different." She finished her salad and set her fork down. "Are you afraid now that she knows you know she'll freak out and run? Are you afraid of the repercussions you could face?"

"I guess." I had a feeling that wouldn't be a problem. She seemed to trust me—really trust me. I had faith this was the beginning to a lifelong relationship. I believed this was the end of the road for me—that I found what Francesca found with Hawke. I believed this was the beginning of my happily ever after. "But I have a good feeling it'll be okay."

***

She eyed my sushi with her chopsticks between her fingertips. Her leg brushed up against mine under the table, giving me a hard-on through our entire meal.

"Want a piece, sweetheart?"

"Well, since you're offering..." She snatched a roll and dropped it into her mouth.

316

"Well, I only offered because I was getting the third degree. But since you're giving me a nice rub under the table I'll give you whatever you want."

"Wow. Too bad my hand can't reach you...wonder what I would get then."

I adjusted my jeans without being discreet about it. Her sexy playfulness was unbelievable. And the most shocking part was, she had no idea just how sexy she was. She didn't even need to try. That sexy lingerie was useless when she already had everything she needed.

She snatched another roll off my plate and took small bites, looking cute as hell.

"I love watching you eat."

"Yeah?" she asked. "I love watching you eat me."

Fuck, she was killing me. "We'll have dessert when we get back to my apartment."

"I look forward to it."

I quickly got the check and slipped the cash inside, wanting to get back into bed as quickly as possible. I had a fiery minx that wanted me, and all of the foreplay we did was intoxicating.

We entered my apartment then immediately headed to the bedroom. Having lunch with Francesca made me realize a grave mistake I made. I told Rose's secret to someone without getting her permission first. Rose would probably never find out that Francesca knew, but I knew I needed to come clean about it. The last time I kept the truth from her we broke up. I didn't want to go down that road again. "Not to kill your engine, but I need to tell you something."

"What?" She pulled her shirt over her head then immediately moved to her bra. Her timid nature had completely disappeared over the course of the month. Now she was comfortable with me in a way she never was before.

I tried to ignore her nakedness and move on. "I know I told you I wouldn't tell anyone your secret but...I told Francesca a few months ago. You and I were broken up and I needed someone to talk to. I'm sorry." I sat at the edge of the bed and put my arms on my knees. This would probably lead to a huge fight. And she would probably walk out on me—not that I wasn't used to it.

"Oh..." She sat beside me, covering her chest with her arms.

"I told her because I wanted her to help me get you back. I'm sorry. I shouldn't have said anything. But I was desperate."

"That means Hawke knows too...?"

"No. " I doubt she would tell him something like that. "I understand if you're upset with me. I told a secret that wasn't mine to tell. I hope you can forgive me."

Instead of being silent and standoffish she sighed. "It's okay, Kyle. I know you meant well."

Say what? "Huh?"

"I said it's okay."

She wasn't going to walk out on me? She wasn't going to yell at me? She was just okay with it? "Are you sure?"

"Yeah." She placed her hand on my thigh. "I know you would never hurt me on purpose."

Somehow, I fell more in love with her. This was the relationship I wanted from the beginning. This kind of trust and understanding was something I always knew we would have. We were perfect together, opposite sides of the same coin. The connection between us ran deep, deeper than anything else. "Thank you."

"Now get those clothes off." She moved into my side and started kissing my neck as she buttoned my shirt.

I felt my heart speed like a train, and I wasn't sure how I'd be able to remain in control tonight. With every passing day it was growing more difficult, more impossible.

Hopefully, I'd make it through tonight.

***

Rose held the blueprint as she looked at the few acres of beach I owned. She was double-checking her measurements, looking at the trajectory of the sun as well as the direction of the wind. "I think it's perfect."

I already knew that before we came out here. "Great. Now we can start building."

"It'll probably take a year to build." She gave me an awkward look, like she wasn't sure if that would upset me.

320

"It's okay. I know these things take time."

She rolled up the blueprint and kept her back to the wind so it wouldn't go flying into the air. "It's a beautiful day today."

"I think it's just you." I wrapped my arm around her as we headed back to the car. "Want to head to the beach house?"

"Sure."

"I'm excited to sleep there with you—not at my mom's." I smiled at her so she knew I was just teasing.

"Who said anything about sleep?" She smiled back when she knew she had me.

My smile immediately dropped.

We drove to my house just a few miles away then walked inside with all of our luggage. It was exactly the same as I left it. I didn't spend as much time at the place as I should, and every time I arrived it felt like another home. "What do you want to do tonight?"

"Other than get naked and make out?"

She was torturing me on purpose. I knew it. "Yes. Other than that."

"Maybe we can make dinner here and sit on the beach."

"That sounds like an excellent idea." *And a PG one.*

***

After we made dinner we sat together on the beach with our feet in the sand. The wind had died down so it was easy to eat the chicken and greens we prepared. We shared a bottle of red wine and looked out at the ocean, cherishing the sunset just before it disappeared over the horizon.

"You're amazing on the grill." She ate all of her food, which was rare for her. Most of the time she just picked at it until it was a mess on her plate.

"Thanks. I get that a lot."

She ate the last piece of roll then set her plate aside. "If I were you, I'd be here all the time."

"Well, I have a lady and a job in the city."

"I guess I should be grateful you don't have a lady out here."

"I can hardly handle the one I've already got." I drank my wine then gave her a playful smile.

"You can definitely handle me, Kyle." Her arm hooked through mine and she kissed me on the cheek.

Somehow, I loved that kiss more than the ones on the mouth. "I love this."

"What?"

"I love how different we are now. I love how you look at me like that. I love the way you touch me. I love the way you need me." I wasn't as verbose about those kinds of things, but with Rose I couldn't stop talking. I wasn't self-conscious to say sissy things.

Her smile disappeared and her face turned serious. "I love it too. You brought me back to life. I feel like the person I used to be, the carefree and happy woman I'd forgotten about."

"I like her. I'm glad I've finally met her."

"She's glad to meet you too."

I rubbed my nose against hers, feeling my heart ache in joy. Even if she didn't realize what we truly were to each other, I was grateful I found the kind of love I'd been looking for. With Francesca, I thought she was the woman of my dreams. But when I met Rose, everything changed. I'd realized that my love for Francesca was pathetic in comparison to the way I felt for Rose. I knew we would get married someday and have two beautiful kids. We'd grow old together, and when we passed away, we'd still be together. Maybe one day she would realize that. I hoped so. "I've waited a long time to meet you. More than you realize."

Her hand tightened around my arm. "Somehow, I feel like we've already met. Or, I feel like I already knew you when I walked into that restaurant. Only someone truly special would have been able to make me fall in love, to trust a man the way I trusted you. I didn't think that was possible...until you."

"I feel the same way. I knew there was something different about you. I didn't just think you were beautiful. And I didn't just think you were interesting. The second I saw you, I knew there was more to it." I wasn't sure if she would ever make the connection, but I certainly did.

"You know who we remind me of?"

"Hmm?"

"Francesca and Hawke."

My fingertips suddenly burned in expectation. "Really? Why?"

She looked down like she was ashamed, or couldn't find the words she wanted to say.

"Sweetheart, tell me."

"It's kind of silly."

I had a feeling it wasn't. "I want to know anyway."

"Well...sometimes I think we're just like them—that we're soul mates." She still wouldn't look at me, afraid of my reaction. "I know that sounds just as crazy as it did when Francesca said it but...I don't think I'd ever be able to be with anyone else but you. Only someone that shares my soul would have put me back together the way you did. Only someone destined to be with me would have gone through the same experiences. Only someone...I was connected with would have been so patient and understanding. I just find it hard to believe that we're just two random people that happened to meet in that restaurant. I feel like our fates were meant to intertwine. I don't think we ever had a choice."

That's what I'd been hoping to hear but never expected it to actually happen. She realized it on her own, that there was something special between us. I didn't have to convince her or make her realize it on her own. She came to the conclusion based on her own thoughts and experiences. "I've known for a while."

She finally met my gaze. "You don't think I'm crazy?"

"No. I knew before we broke up. I think I knew the moment I saw you. It wasn't love at first sight. It was something more than that."

Her eyes slowly coated with tears. "Really? You aren't just saying that?"

"No. Never."

"Kyle..."

Both of my hands slid up her cheeks until I cupped her face. Then I pressed our foreheads together, treasuring the moment as a single person.

Then she began to cry. "I didn't think I'd ever be okay again...I didn't think I'd ever be put back together.

You're the reason I'm here now. You're the reason I'm so happy."

"Sweetheart..." It was painful to listen to her cry, but since they were happy tears it wasn't so excruciating. "You put me back together too. You fixed me just as much as I fixed you."

She pressed her face into my chest and pressed her body as close to mine as possible. The waves crashed in the distance, and the sound of distant seagulls was distantly heard. But it felt like it was just the two of us— two halves of a single soul.

***

I wasn't nervous at all.

There wasn't a single doubt.

Nothing held me back.

We went into my bedroom and immediately began to undress. I sensed Rose understood this night would be different than all the others. She didn't know what I'd been waiting for, but now she knew I was ready to move to the next level, to finally take the last step.

I didn't kiss her like I usually did. I took my time undressing her, letting her clothes slip through my fingers until they hit the floor. Our breathing was heightened because everything else was so silent. As more of her body was revealed all I could think about was how beautiful she was—and that she was mine.

She was just mine.

I guided her to the bed then moved on top of her. I'd already made love to her before, and it was beautiful and satisfying. But it felt like the first time all over again— because this was the beginning of forever.

Our kisses started off slow, and she slowly wrapped her legs around my waist. I loved it when she squeezed my hips, like she was anxious for me. I knew I found my future wife, and that's what made this night so special. I never knew how much I wanted to be in love, to be committed to a single person, until she walked into my life.

There was a stack of condoms in my drawer, and I felt guilty for having them there. They were for the girls I hooked up with over the weekend. They were usually gone by Sunday night. To use something I'd planted for all the others simply didn't feel right. I didn't know this was when Rose would make the realization, but I should have planned for it anyway.

But I didn't have a choice.

She wasn't on birth control and I didn't want to do the pull out method. It wasn't exactly romantic at the end, getting my seed all over her stomach. Maybe if we'd been making love for a while it'd be okay, but not tonight. Without any other option, I opened the nightstand and snatched a condom.

She kissed my neck and shoulders as I ripped it from the foil. My dick was rock-hard and excited to be inside her. I'd been there once before, and there was nothing quite like it.

Her small fingers wrapped around my wrist. "Can we not use one? I want to feel you."

When she talked like that I went a little crazy. "I don't have anything else…"

"I'm on the pill."

Since when? "You are?"

She nodded.

I had a million questions to ask but I knew now wasn't the right time. I tossed the condom on the ground and returned my focus to her. I positioned one of her beautiful legs over my shoulder and leaned far over her, our foreheads touching. I'd never been with a sexier woman in my life, and I couldn't wait to have her. "I've never made love to a more beautiful woman..."

Her nails dug into my arms, and a quiet gasp escaped her lips.

I slowly inserted myself, going as slow as possible. I knew she was okay, that this interaction didn't remind her of anything painful. All she thought about was me and how much I loved her. It didn't elicit any painful memories—only beautiful ones.

When I was completely inside her she released a gasp of pleasure. "Kyle..."

I let her body get used to me for a moment. I kissed her slowly and massaged her clitoris with my thumb, keeping her as relaxed and aroused as possible. I wasn't full of myself, but I knew I was pretty endowed below.

And she was tight.

She breathed quickly into my mouth, her nails still digging into me.

I slowly thrust into her, our eyes on each other. Sex was always good with my partners, but it reached a new level with her. All she did was lay underneath me and it was still amazing. I loved feeling my dick stroke her, moving in and out. I loved how soaked she was. I made her feel this way. I made her give life and love a second chance.

"It feels really good…"

I felt a groan in the back of my throat. "It does."

"Harder." She grabbed my hip and yanked on me.

I moved into her faster but didn't give it to her hard. There would be time for hard and fast sex later, the kind that happened in the shower or in the back of a car. But for tonight, it was just sweet lovemaking. I didn't want anything else.

"Thank you for not giving up on me."

My thrusts faltered before I kept going. "Never."

Her hands moved to my shoulders, and she gripped me tightly, never letting me go. She rocked her hips below me, sliding my cock in and out of her as we moved together. It felt right—moving with her.

I already wanted to come. I could usually go for a long time when I was with a woman but now it was a struggle. I knew it had nothing to do with my abstinence. It had to do with the woman underneath me, wanting me and loving me.

"I'm gonna come..." Her breathing grew more labored and deep. Sweat formed on her chest and rubbed against me every time I moved. I could feel her tighten around me, her climax quickly approaching.

I was excited to feel her come all over my dick.

She gripped my shoulders and rocked herself into me harder, moaning incoherently through her lips. "Yes..." Her eyes lit up in flames, and her mouth formed a sexy O.

I couldn't hold on for a moment longer. Seeing her explode underneath me made me want to do the same. Our first time together wouldn't last long, but we had the rest of the night to make up for it. "Sweetheart." I felt the explosion start deep inside me before it reached everywhere else. It burned me alive but felt so good at the same time. I pumped into her, filling her with everything I had.

Her eyes were locked to mine as I finished. The unspoken question was there. She didn't need to ask it because I could read her mind so well. It was an ability I acquired a long time ago.

I gave her a long kiss before I answered. "All I saw was you."

Sunday

EPILOGUE

Kyle

When I woke up I could hear the ocean. The waves were breaking once they hit the shore, and the seagulls were crying loudly as they looked for seafood that washed up with the tide. The sunlight filtered through the open window, the curtain slowly swaying in the breeze.

I opened my eyes and squinted when I saw the light.

The sheets were soft around my body, just washed the previous day. The scent of lavender filled my bedroom, the product of a woman's touch. I managed to force my body to cooperate and look around.

Rose wasn't there.

The bathroom door was closed, and the faucet turned on then off again. I kicked the sheets back then walked across the room. I wore my pajama bottoms but lacked a shirt. Without knocking I turned the knob and opened the door.

Standing there in one of my t-shirts was the love of my life.

She turned to me with her toothbrush still in her mouth. A mischievous look was in her eyes, like she knew exactly how upset I would be when I woke up to her absence. She brushed her teeth a few more seconds before she spit into the sink. "Morning."

"Morning, sweetheart." I wrapped my arms around her waist and pulled her shirt up, revealing her glorious ass in a black thong. My hand rubbed one bare cheek, and I placed a kiss on her neck.

She watched my actions in the mirror, the toothbrush still in her mouth.

I grabbed both of her ass cheeks with my hands and gave them a firm squeeze. "How'd you sleep?"

She brushed her teeth for another minute before she spit. "Good."

"I slept really well until I woke up to a nightmare." The corner of her lip moved up

I yanked the toothbrush out of her grasp and tossed it on the counter. Then I gripped her and positioned her on the surface, her legs wrapped around my waist. She automatically hooked her arms around my neck like she'd been expecting my advance.

I gripped her lower back and gave her a slow kiss, one that immediately turned heated and sexy. I sucked her bottom lip before I felt her small tongue in my mouth. They danced together seductively, making the temperature raise a few degrees. My dick was hard the moment I opened my eyes, and I suspected her pussy had become wet since I opened the door.

I pulled down the front of my sweatpants and revealed my long cock. I quickly adjusted her thong then slipped my length inside. My prediction was right. She was definitely wet.

She tried to hold back the moan that escaped her lips but it was futile. "Oh, yes."

I moved into her on the bathroom counter, the mirror right in front of me. I watched myself move inside her before I turned my gaze back to her. I gripped her by the chin possessively and turned her face, forcing her to look in the reflection. "Watch me fuck you."

Her hand gripped my ass, and she pulled me further into her, moaning uncontrollably. She was slick and tight, the perfect counterpart to my thick length. "Kyle..."

I loved hearing her say my name.

I rocked my hips harder, giving it to her at a quicker pace. I kept my grip on her chin, forcing her to watch me enjoy her. She always came apart when we made love. She had a greater sexual appetite than I did— if you could believe it.

"I'm gonna come..." She dug her nails further into my ass, tightening noticeably.

"Yes." There was no greater pleasure than giving pleasure. I loved seeing her eyes roll back in her head. I loved the perfect little O she made with her dirty mouth. I loved the way she came undone for me, unsure what to do when that climax hit her like a freight train. "Come for me."

"God..."

"Mommy?"

Rose and I both stopped in mid thrust. Our eyes locked and alarm shot through us. The amazing sex we were just having turned ice-cold.

Fuck.

Rose cleared her throat. "Mommy will be right out."

"Where's Daddy?"

I pulled out of Rose and quickly pulled on my sweatpants. "I'm right here, Son. We'll be out in a second."

Rose hopped off the counter then quickly adjusted herself.

I grabbed a toothbrush and shoved it into my mouth before I opened the door. "Hey, tiger. Good morning." I pulled out the toothbrush and tried to act natural.

Cole seemed oblivious to what his parents were doing five seconds ago. Perhaps he was naïve, or perhaps he was just too young to understand. He was only five years old. "Can we go find seashells today?"

"Absolutely. Make sure your sister is ready."

He made a disgusted face. "Does she have to come?"

"Of course she does," I said. "She's your sister."

"But she picks her nose all the time..." He crossed his arms over his chest.

"Like you didn't pick your nose?" Rose teased.

"But she wipes them on me!" Cole stomped his foot.

"Then wipe yours on her," I said. "You'll be even."

"Yuck!" Cole grimaced all over again.

I kneeled down and rustled his hair like I always did. "Give me five minutes alright?"

He pouted his lips. "Every time you say five minutes it's a lot longer."

Maybe he wasn't as naïve as I hoped. "I promise. Besides, we have company coming over soon."

"Who?" Cole asked.

"Aunt Francesca and Uncle Hawke."

"Are the girls coming too?" Cole asked.

"Yep," Rose answered. "And you better be nice to Suzie. No more picking on her."

Cole rolled his eyes and left the bedroom.

I shut the bathroom door and locked it this time. "Now where were we?"

Rose grabbed her toothbrush. "You promised him five minutes."

"And I'll be ready in five minutes."

"Not if we pick up where we left off."

"Consider it a challenge." I returned her to the counter and positioned myself between her legs. "Can I make my wife come in five minutes or less?"

"You've done it before."

I slipped my dick inside her and made her expression change. Her eyes had a dreamy look to them, and her lips parted in a sexy way. "And I'll do it again."

Sunday

Want To Stalk Me?

Subscribe to my newsletter for updates on new releases, giveaways, and for my comical monthly newsletter. You'll get all the dirt you need to know. Sign up today.

www.eltoddbooks.com

Facebook:

https://www.facebook.com/ELTodd42

Twitter:

@E_L_Todd

Now you have no reason not to stalk me. You better get on that.

EL's Elites

I know I'm lucky enough to have super fans, you know, the kind that would dive off a cliff for you. They have my back through and through. They love my books and they love spreading the word. Their biggest goal is to see me on the New York Times bestsellers list and they'll stop at nothing to make it happen. While it's a lot of work, it's also a lot of fun. What better way to make friendships than to connect with people who love the same thing you do?

Are you one of these super fans?

If so, send a request to join the Facebook group. It's closed so you'll have a hard time finding it without the link. Here it is:

https://www.facebook.com/groups/119232692078437 3/

Hope to see you there, ELITE!

Printed in Great Britain
by Amazon

83890877R00199